Editor-in-Chief
Lena Kraus

Executive Editor
Carly Craig

Art Director
Amos O'Connor

Financial Coordinator
Julia Guillermina

Workshop Coordinator
Wren True

Website Manager
Juliann Guerra

Blog Coordinator
Katie Hay-Molopo

Event Managers
Katie Hay-Molopo
Tess Simpson

Social Media Managers
Beverley Thornton
Wren True

Carly Craig
Katie Hay-Molopo
Miriam Huxley

Editors
Hayley Bernier
Nicole Christine Caratas
Anthi Cheimariou
Carly Craig
Katie Hay-Molopo
Katharina Körber
Lena Kraus
Alyssa Osiecki
Alice Rogers
Tess Simpson
Elena Sims
Gerry Stewart
Wren True
Hanna-Maria Vester

Proofreaders
Anthi Cheimariou
Carly Craig
Lena Kraus
Dorothy Lawrenson
Elena Sims
Katharina Körber

FOREWORD

Welcome to *Hillfire Anthology Volume Three*! This is a milestone I couldn't know we would reach when we started out in 2022. It is a small one, but it feels significant. We've made it this far; we're here to stay.

I'm very excited to share this beautiful book with you. This volume saw some changes to the team as friends and fellow contributors continued on their journeys. It is an honour to witness our members growing, as writers, as artists, as project managers, professionals, humans. If you bought this book, you have helped us to keep doing what we do. We are sincerely grateful. Thank you!

The Hillfire journey started in Edinburgh, where most of us met during our various creative writing degrees. This year, we were able to open our community to external applications for the first time. It's been an absolute pleasure to see this project grow and evolve. At the heart of what we do is our tried and trusted process, with all authors workshopping each other's writing in addition to our team's edits. We focus on collaboration, working together to make each piece the best it can be. Each is an essential part of the tapestry that is the finished anthology. When I was looking for a name for this press, I thought about Arthur's Seat, the iconic hill in Edinburgh's Holyrood Park. In spring, yellow gorse flowers light up the whole hillside so bright you can see it from miles away. I love how the small flowers on those extraordinarily spiky bushes can create such a spectacular effect together. This is what I'm aiming for with Hillfire: to collect pieces of writing that burn even brighter in combination.

Art can make people see the truth, sense it, without ever directly addressing it. It can also communicate truths in more direct ways, like one of the poems, "June 2023", which addresses fascist tendencies gathering strength, legally, from within our democratic systems. Democracies are fragile. Life as we know it is fragile. This year, temperatures globally have risen by above 1.5°C for the first time. People are coming together to defend our rights and our future, creating hope. Strikes and protests are an essential part of functional democracies, one way our human rights and our livelihoods can be protected and defended. But our rights to strike and protest have been threatened here in the UK and globally. These demonstrations are tools with which many of our human rights have been won, and an attack on them is an attack on our human rights. This continues to be our shared responsibility.

While we're doing this work, it is essential to rest and take care of ourselves and each other. Art can be both food for thought and welcome escape. I hope you find some of both in these pages.

We don't do themed volumes at Hillfire, and yet it seems that in this anthology, we have an above-average number of stories involving boats. Just like boats can carry you from one place to another, we hope the writing in this volume opens up new perspectives. We can't wait to have you along on this journey!

Lena Kraus
Founder, Editor-in-Chief

A NOTE ON THIS BOOK

This book has been produced by writers from many places, which is reflected in different varieties of English.

We have included content identifiers in the table of contents, much like allergens on a menu. If there are topics you don't want to read about, we have hopefully provided you with a means to avoid them. Please don't hesitate to reach out to us if you have any questions or concerns about specific content.

CONTENTS

Carly Craig	3	Stay on the Boat
Alexandra Ye	11	The Garden Party
E Mardot	16	There's Something About[†*‖]
Hanna-Maria Vester	23	Secret Agents
Hanna-Maria Vester	27	In June of 2023[#]
Dorothy Lawrenson	29	The Highwayman[‡]
Malina Shamsudin	35	The Huff Puff Hustle
David Blakeslee	41	Generation
Nicole Christine Caratas	47	Last Lie[‖]
Gerry Stewart	51	Night Turnings
Gerry Stewart	53	Pentecost
Gerry Stewart	54	Evening River Swim at Ansku Sauna
Emerson Rose Craig	56	Resume
Anthi Cheimariou	62	Blind World
Anthi Cheimariou	63	Words
Anthi Cheimariou	64	Amygdala Hijack – Oxytocin
Katie Hay-Molopo	66	The Art of Delivery[Δ]
Miriam Huxley	72	Tsk, Tsk
Thomas Carroll	78	Boat///House[§]
Skye Wilson	83	Epithalamion i

Skye Wilson	84	Elegy i
Skye Wilson	85	Epithalamion ii
M.H. Monica	86	Hey Eve
Tess Simpson	91	The Witch Bone ∆ ∞ ‖
Katharina Körber	96	Self-Portrait as Translation
Katharina Körber	98	Grandmother's Garden
Katharina Körber	99	Rheumatoid Android ‡
Megan Willis	100	Vague Prophecy ‡
Abigail O'Neill	107	Cinnamon Rolls
Yang Yue	114	The Posthumous Letter ◊ ‡ ¶
Julia Guillermina	121	;)
Alex Penland	127	Clockstride ‖
Alyssa Osiecki	130	Ghost Towns
Hayley Bernier	135	To Love as an Obsessive Thinker*
Hayley Bernier	136	That First Call
Hayley Bernier	138	Something is Moving Up There
Wren True	139	Magwarth ∞

CONTENT IDENTIFIERS

Death *   Alcohol abuse †   Medical details ‡

War §   Suicide ¶   Murder‖   Gore ∞

Bigotry #   Childbirth ∆   Incest ◊

CARLY CRAIG

Stay on the Boat

"Rule Number One: Stay on the boat.
"Rule Number Two: Stay on the boat.
"Rule Number Three: Always wear your—I'm just kidding. Stay on the goddamn boat."

Hannah had laughed. The sun was shining and the sea was calm—a glorious day to embark on the last great adventure of her twenties. All that stood between the crew and the open ocean—pure freedom, in Hannah's eyes—were a few remaining formalities.

"I know it sounds obvious," Alice pressed on, "but I need to drive this home." Despite her wry smile, under Alice's short-cropped, sandy gray hair, her eyes were serious. "They say that falling overboard in open water is like jumping out of a plane without a parachute. Do you understand? If you go off the boat, you're as good as dead."

***

Ten.

Hannah is blinded. Pain wracks her chest, all-consuming. Saltwater spews from her nose and mouth. Disoriented, she thrashes her arms and gasps for air.

*

On deck, Alice is shouting.

Jamie emerges from the cabin, wild-eyed. "What happened?"

"Get the buoy in the water and—here—take the spotlight," Alice orders.

"Shit, Alice. Holy shit."

"We have ten minutes."

*

Nine.

Hannah doesn't remember the buoyancy aid inflating, but now, its reflective plastic digs into her shoulders and presses against her frozen cheeks as the waves drag her skyward into the stormy night air and plunge her down again. Rain and seafoam spatter her from all directions. It's hard to open her eyes, hard to breathe. Her lungs burn.

*

"Do you have eyes on her?" Jamie wrenches the man overboard buoy from its mount on the guardrail and heaves it into the sea. On contact with the water, the neon yellow device spills orange smoke into the heavy air.

Jamie scrambles across the undulating deck, gathering and jettisoning anything that will float: cushions, a few loose water bottles, a spare life jacket, a bag of bread.

At the helm, Alice fights the swell and struggles to point the boat into the wind.

"Alice, *eyes?*"

"Not anymore, no. Get the bins from inside. Watch for a light."

Jamie dashes back into the cabin.

*

Eight.

Hannah kicks and spins, eyes darting in search of any sign of the boat, anything other than unbroken waves in every direction. The only thought her cold-shocked mind can muster is: No.

Then, her gaze alights on her shoulder, where the emergency locator beacon on her buoyancy aid has auto-deployed its little yellow antenna. It emits a blip of green light at regular intervals. She tries to focus on this steady beat and slow her breathing.

*

With the bow in the wind, Alice reactivates the autopilot and clips her buoyancy aid to the lifeline.

Jamie bursts back through the cabin doors with a pair of binoculars.

"The mainsail's jammed," Alice says. "I'm gonna need to find a way to bring it down. Keep looking." She steps out of the helm station and crouches low, right hand on the guardrail and left hand on the roof of the cabin as she creeps forward across the upper deck toward the mast. The world rolls around her.

Jamie stations herself on the back deck, wrapping one arm around a roof pillar to keep steady. The red lights on the man overboard buoy cut through the thick, oppressive murk. The mist muddies her sense of distance, but as she registers how far the current has already dragged the device, a wave of nausea floods her stomach.

***

Seven.

All is dark, fogged out. The world is unreal. The air is water. The boat is gone.

It feels like the dread pooling in Hannah's lungs might drown her before the sea gets a fair chance. Her foul weather gear is already soaked through, stiff and heavy on her limbs. Her body quakes.

***

Up at the mast, Alice heaves on the downhaul. With the torrential rain in her eyes, she can't see a snag anywhere, but the rope and the mainsail won't budge. The boat pitches like a see-saw and a wall of spray nearly sweeps Alice off her feet as they surf down one wave and bury their bow in the next.

She wants to scream. She wants to cry. She wants to fall over and pin her head between her knees and shut it all out. "FUCK!" she roars back at the storm.

All this, happening on her watch. No matter how many stories she had heard from friends, on forums, in magazines—she never really believed it was possible. Stupid. She bites her lip—hard. Tastes blood in her mouth. Adjusts her grip on the rope and throws all her weight against it.

⁂

Six.

In her head, Hannah keeps circling through the order of events, as though, by pinpointing exactly where everything went wrong, she might be able to save herself.

There was a squall. Worse than expected.

They decided to drop the mainsail, but something got stuck.

She clipped in—yes, she's sure, she must have—and went to fix it. And then. A sudden wind shift. A jibe. A violent impact.

Now, this, the cold, like needles all over her skin, stabbing, pressing deeper into her core.

There was a squall. Worse than expected. If they had known, they would have dropped the mainsail earlier. But they didn't, and then they tried, and then something stuck, so—yes—she clipped in, and what else? What else could they possibly have done?

***

Alice finds it. A snag, not up the mast, thank god, but in a mangled pulley biting into the main halyard and trapping the sail in place. Her first thought is to find a screwdriver, but no—no time. Instead, she grabs the safety knife from its lanyard around her neck, unsheathes it, and sets its saw-toothed blade to work. The rope gives way in one sharp snap of tension, and then the sail is free.

"We're a go!" Alice screams over the wind to Jamie. She slides down the cabin roof and staggers back toward the helm.

***

Five.

Everything is heavy. Her head on her neck. Her arms floating at her sides. Hannah tries to flex her fingers. They barely move. Ten minutes, Alice warned them. Ten minutes in these waters before the cold renders you unconscious, or worse. The beacon pulses like a slow heartbeat. Hannah begins to cry.

And then, Alice is back at the helm and firing up the engines. Her eyes fix on two green markers on the nav screen. "Jamie?" Her voice breaks.

"What's the plan?" Jamie shouts, binoculars trained on the swell. The man overboard buoy has slipped away into the storm and out of sight.

"I see her on the AIS. I'm bringing us around. Watch off the bow."

"Thank fuck. How far is she?"

Too far, Alice thinks. Her head feels fizzy with adrenaline, explosive. Her heart pounds in her throat. "We'll get there," she hears herself promise.

※

Four.

Hannah isn't shivering anymore. She remembers vaguely that this is a "bad sign." But they say cold isn't the worst way to go, and—yes, well, actually. There are things: the once-sharp pain in her chest feels better— what was it that happened to it? A crashing wave, a swinging boom, water, everywhere. So cold, and, but, not. Not anymore.

Stay awake.

There are things maybe she hasn't done. But. It's just sort of warm, and sleepy…

Stop it.

There are things, like, maybe she spent too much time worrying—or was it not enough? Why worry when there is nothing I can do. Ha. But look. Look, Hannah.

And she does, blinking hard and then opening her eyes as wide as she can manage. She looks at the looming shapes each obsidian wave forms against the charcoal sky. She looks at the thousands of little splashes made by raindrops colliding with the ocean's surface. She looks at her own two hands, her fingers terribly white where they poke out of her fingerless gloves, but there, still there. She looks at—

⁂

Alice watches the AIS and Jamie watches the water. Both engines are on full power as they chase a small, green-glowing icon on their nav screen. Still, they are fighting the drag of the wind and the waves, and as they move, so too does their crewmate's transmitter, still too far away. A heavy silence falls between them.

⁂

Three.

—there. Just there. A pinprick of light.

ALEXANDRA YE

The Garden Party

Everyone arrived at Joanna's party dressed for something like an Easter service, or a cousin's high school graduation ceremony—clad in linen jackets, or garments with puffed sleeves. I was wearing a floaty jumpsuit I had purchased especially for the occasion, because I feared bloating into my pants. It didn't matter how high-waisted they were; pants caused me the ultimate gastrointestinal distress, even though everyone else wore pants in public and seemed somehow to be fine.

I had brought a bottle of wine. It felt very important that there was enough wine. I was never really comfortable around the people Joanna had invited, who were ostensibly my friends. It seemed I spent time with them the same way I ate olives, or ordered coffee; I didn't like either, but others were so enthusiastic in their partaking that I had to keep nibbling and taking sips, each time, just in case I started enjoying the taste.

Through Joanna's garden, there was soft grass and bushes bursting with peonies and a table set with a gingham cloth. I sometimes found it difficult not to be cynical about everything. Was she trying to grow her Instagram following? Or was she just rich? We already knew she was rich; she had a garden.

It was hard not to resent Joanna, who stood at the

head of the table in an orange frock, opening a bottle of prosecco. But when I took my seat and selected a cube of cheese from the little heap in front of me and bit into its spectacularly firm yet creamy form, the meanness in me seemed to dissolve. The cork eased out from the prosecco bottle, releasing a gentle hiss. Now Joanna was running out enormous platters of salmon kebabs, garnished with lemons and herbs and pomegranate seeds; followed by radish salad, and bowls of buttered corn, crying over and over again, "No!—Sit down!—I've got it!"—and Andrea was pouring tremendous quantities of wine, the prosecco fizzling flirtatiously in our glasses.

We ate until the sun was low in the trees. The candle flames bloomed in the air. It was a warm night. You could smell smoke from someone grilling down the street and hear bits of music drifting over from the passing cars. For a sudden, mad moment, I desperately wished I was in love with somebody. For once, I'd have given anything to suffer a crush again, one of those really severe ones in middle school, when you'd sit behind someone on the bus every day wishing for them to please, please, drop a pencil so that it rolls to your feet and you can hand it back. I never wanted anything that badly anymore. It had all taken on a practical dimension, at some point. My eyes flicked from Helen to Grace to Noah and back to Helen, and I knew with utter certainty that if any of them had propositioned me in that moment, I'd have instantly accepted and then committed to an exclusive relationship of at least one year. It was with this mindset that I entered the surrounding conversation. They were talking about how mentally ill their parents were.

"It's like you're watching someone disappear," said Grace, whose father was an alcoholic. We all nodded sympathetically. On the other end of the table, where Joanna was sitting, someone said something funny and there was a prolonged outburst of honking laughter. I looked over and tried not to appear too interested.

"And there's nothing you can do even when you see them all the time," Noah was saying. His mother had depression, he said, and she was never going to acknowledge its existence, much less seek help for it, because of cultural stigmas. He shrugged and shook his head. There was a brief silence, and we all sipped from our glasses.

I was enjoying the wine very much. Only I wished I was sitting on the other end of the table, where another wild explosion of laughter was occurring. I looked over and saw that Joanna was pulling her hair in front of her face in faux embarrassment. Andrea was enthusiastically gesturing with a fork. Mariam made eye contact and then came over with more wine. She was hiccupping from laughing so hard, but she let it bubble out when she sensed the somber mood and quickly returned to the other side of the table. It was a long table. There was enough room to accommodate disparate moods, and we often ended up telling each other intimate facts about ourselves just to simulate a feeling of closeness.

Now Grace, Helen and Noah were talking about their various attachment styles, and how they had been shaped by their parents' mental illnesses. I thought about my own parents. My dad had atrial fibrillation but that was all, they were otherwise both exceedingly healthy. I had experienced a very pleasant childhood of great happiness and security. So much so that, as a child, I had fantasized frequently about becoming an orphan. I'd imagine it happening in such detail that I could smell the stale cigarettes and old coffee cups from the backseat of the car when the state authorities came to pick me up. They'd drive me away from my empty house and I would cry softly, because I was all alone in the world, and I would see in the rearview mirror the adults exchanging grim, piteous looks. This fantasy often moved me so deeply that I would sob in the shower – for myself, and for my two dead parents, at least until my mother opened the bathroom door and shouted: "What's taking you so long? The walls are molding because you never turn on the fan!" I considered sharing my orphan fantasy with the table but it was already too late; they were talking about abusive relationships now.

The lower region of my jumpsuit was feeling rather tight, even though it was a silky jumpsuit with culotte legs. I excused myself from the table and went inside to find the bathroom, hoping nobody would notice how drunkenly I was shuffling through the grass. When I sat down on the toilet, my thighs immediately stuck to the seat. Nonetheless, it was a relief. My jumpsuit was in a puddle around my ankles, and the rest of my body was entirely naked. I couldn't tell if I felt vulnerable or sexy. I'd watched a YouTube video once about how to be hot and the girl had said you should sleep naked because it will make you feel sexy. Maybe this was the same principle, except I was peeing. Maybe tonight I should seduce somebody. Noah would be an easy target. I remembered now that Noah's father had recently died of cancer. Thank god I hadn't shared my orphan fantasy. I looked down and saw that my pubic hairs had grown so long on each side that they thatched together in the middle, like the top of a campfire, and then I felt awash with shame. I felt disgusting. I was a bad person with no real friends, and I had never appreciated my wonderful family, even though they loved me more than anything. Maybe this was why I had a weak character and a bad disposition. It had been weeks since I'd called. I reached into the culottes puddle to fish out my phone.

"Hi, honey," my mother said when she picked up.

"Hi, ma."

"Is everything alright?" There was another peal of laughter from the table outside. I felt a flash of annoyance at my mother's concerned tone.

"Of course everything's alright," I said.

"Okay," she said hesitantly.

"Everything's great," I said. "I'm at a dinner party. In a garden."

"Oh—that sounds lovely."

There was a long pause. "Just hope you and dad are having a nice night," I tried to say.

"Thanks, honey," she said. There was a pause. "Are you okay? Do you need us to come get you or something?"

"Jesus," I said, because I was twenty-three years old and a four-hour drive away. "Don't be fucking ridiculous."

"Well—" she said, and then I hung up. I flushed the toilet, pulled up my jumpsuit, and then went out to the kitchen. Joanna was in there, standing over a pavlova, with a floral apron tied over her dress.

Here we go again, I thought, preparing to twist my face into an obliging smile.

But before I could, Joanna asked me: "What are you looking for?" Her thin voice was full of care. It caught me by surprise; my stupid little mind had to reel to a halt. I don't know, I almost said—I don't know. But then I thought better, regained my sense of irony, and said "Oh, nothing! Nothing! Nothing!"

E MARDOT

There's Something About

Adrian

There was always something about Henry Raine that made him an extremely punchable kind of person. Not killable though, and yet that's exactly what I did.

I sit across from him at our dining table with a bottle of whisky in hand and am about four stages into grief or shock, or whatever the hell emotion makes you prop your dead flatmate into a chair and put a pair of sunglasses over his face. Mostly because I can't bear the thought that under those eyelids his pupils have probably shrouded a pearly grey *and fucking hell, I've killed Henry. I'm a murderer.*

I grab at my hair and slide all the way down until it's chin against wood, choking on another swig of liquor as I go.

It wasn't on purpose – the killing part. And definitely not sober.

We were having another screaming match in the flat, although I don't even know *what* we were arguing about this time. Maybe because it was only five pm and I was already halfway through my second bottle, or the fact I had missed rugby practice for the fourth time in a row.

Honestly, why couldn't Henry be like everyone else in my life who had granted me the mercy of not bothering?

But then, there was always something about Henry that didn't let him leave you alone. All the bloody time. Maybe that's why I punched him when he barged into the room and tried to drag me off the sofa. Maybe it's because he was always just so unrelentingly *there,* and I was sick of it. Sick of those blue eyes falling over my face with concern. A blue that managed to seep through the cracks of my smile whenever we were out with the boys, into the bruises and sores of the last couple months since Mum died.

The weeks where I let the sofa swallow me up the way it did time, watching television for hours, maybe even days. I hated how Henry would get home and interrupt it all with a flick of his hand on the light switch, his other carrying a takeaway bag. His voice a gentle hum that would soak into the noise, into the very cushions tucked beneath me, accompanied by soft palms sliding over my calves as he moved my legs to sit. Henry was the size of a skyscraper and yet he had hands so careful they could probably spin spiderwebs or build snowflakes.

When I punched him earlier, his head had snapped back, legs crumpling in one go. I hadn't thought I'd hit him that hard, but the whisky was already pulling on my limbs and then suddenly there he was on the floor. Before I knew it, I was falling down too. Bawling my eyes out for having killed someone, but not just anyone. It was Henry, sprawled and silent with blood smearing his forehead red, his body so stiff I swear for a moment he even had a boner. I heard that can happen to corpses, so I ignored it out of decency for the dead.

Dead.

I look at him now across the table. His chestnut hair falls over a relaxed brow, broad shoulders slumped against the wall like he's sleeping. Like this is all a dream and not a bloody nightmare. My eyes fall onto those damn hands on the tabletop. My throat tightens and I try to swallow but it's suffocating. There's too much lodged inside.

Henry is dead, and I hate him so much for it.

'I love you,' my mouth says instead. 'I love you, Henry.'

And then I cry even harder because *fuck*, it's true.

Henry

I'm not insane for pretending to be dead for five hours, although I'm sure it looks that way. I just missed my chance to open my eyes is all, and then the night tumbled away like a smashed pianist on a severely out-of-tune piano.

Adrian sits hunched over the table; cheek plastered heavy against the hard surface. His finger taps a hollow rhythm on the whisky bottle in front of him. He's been going at it nonstop since early evening. Every time he staggers up and into the kitchen, I take a long drink from it. At this rate, the man is actively trying to make real corpses out of the two of us.

All of this is Adrian's fault to begin with. I hadn't expected him to swoop to the floor and start crying earlier. I've never seen him shed a tear, not even when he came back from his mother's funeral. Honestly, I was too shocked to say anything when he embraced me on the floor, his hands all over my body, palms brushing every inch of skin until suddenly I wasn't so limp and very much preferred that I would die right then.

'I love you, Henry,' he said an hour ago.

Leave it to Adrian to have to kill someone before

he realises he's in love with them. He's never been the smartest one in the room. (You'd think he would have checked my pulse by now.) (I'm *breathing* for fuck's sake.) Although, I've never admitted I've been in love with him ever since the first time his smile stampeded into my peripheral. But then, everyone falls a little in love with Adrian. He's the type of person with a face that breaks out like sunshine whenever he sees you, whether you're his closest friend or a stranger on the street.

Until his mother died. Then Adrian went from warm summer days to shutting himself up like storm windows. Only he failed to realise he had closed the rain inside along with him. I saw it though, in his strained smiles and glances that never quite met the eye. In the way his body barely dragged past the sofa most days. Or how the bottles began collecting like little heartbreaks in the corner. And for *fuck's sake* his mother died two months ago and here I am letting him have some sort of mental break. Although, strange choice his first move as a murderer was to put me in a chair and sit across from me.

My head is spinning, tongue a bitter rock pressing against the roof of my mouth. I want to take off these ridiculous sunglasses. Instead, I watch as Adrian sinks further into his chair. His face is a rough sketch of furrowed brows, quivering lips – grief for the dead. He's worn that look as long as the filthy grey jumper on his back, shoved over sagging shoulders and rarely taken off since. It makes me want to open my eyes and show him I'm alive. To wipe that expression away entirely. But there's the 'and then' that's terrifying me. Because what if he said, 'I love you' only because he thinks I'm dead? What if it's just that?

What if I come back to life, and suddenly, it's the opposite?

Adrian

I put a couple of playing cards into Henry's palm, a set in front of me too. I don't know why. I'll call the police in the morning to take me. For now, I just want to sit. I think I feel his fingers twitch, but it's most likely my legs jamming against the table as I pull his sunglasses off. I want to glimpse his eyes, that endless blue like the ocean. So expansive, it engulfs you completely. I've been avoiding them for months, and I know it.

'Because you're too good at seeing me,' I say, or think I say.

My chest is a furnace, my eyelids sliding down like thick honey. I pry them open to look at him. I want to see those eyes wash over me again. I really do.

But they won't. And it's all my fault.

Henry

I could open my eyes right now as he puts playing cards into my palm (why the cards, Adrian?) and then he'd probably shoot up like he's spotted a snake in a hole. Startled back until he falls out of his chair altogether. He said he loved me, but there's a chance it's the shock. Or most definitely the alcohol. This is silly. I can't be a corpse forever unless I let myself sit here until I actually die. I deserve it. I can't imagine what he's thinking.

My eyelids flutter to catch a glimpse. I wish I had those blasted shades back on my face. I wonder what expression he's making.

'Even dead you're obnoxiously handsome,' he slurs, and I want to snort in laughter, or more strongly, cry. There's something about Adrian that makes you want to pull him close but trying to catch him is like trying to grasp a ray of sunlight. It comes to you, but you can't make it stay. What if Adrian doesn't stay?

I could open my eyes. But I don't.

Adrian

'I'm not going to kiss you,' I say because a corpse can't consent and I don't want Henry to think I'm taking advantage of him in death. Especially if his ghost is hanging around. If they do that sort of thing. There's something about Henry that makes me think he would definitely be a lingering spirit. But then, he was the type of person you couldn't help wanting to keep close by.

I feel like Icarus plummeting into the ocean. A catastrophe of salt and sea and swollen lungs, realising too late that the deep blue would have cradled me to safety, if only I had stopped thrashing about.

My fingers brush lightly against Henry's. I swear he's almost warm.

'I just want to see your eyes.'

Henry

Adrian's hand is over mine, bittersweet breath on my cheek. I don't know what he's doing but he's getting closer.

'I just want to see your eyes,' he says, and I hear him stumble, catching himself with a clumsy slap of his palms against the table. It rattles and, playing a proper dead person or maybe I'm just past drunk, my head flops forward. I feel sick. Everything is spinning.

Warm hands cup either side of my face.

'Even if they're cloudy white,' he murmurs. 'Is it okay if I look?'

I could open my eyes right now. It seems like Adrian's going to do it anyway. If I fling them open though, I might give him a heart attack. He's never been this close before.

He said he loved me, but it could be a mistake. My head is spinning. His hands are hot. He said he loved me and even if he doesn't, I don't want him to feel guilty because I'm not dead. And I do love him. All I've wanted the past few months is for Adrian to take my hand and get off that damn sofa. Well, he's off it now.

'I love you, Henry.' His voice is a high whine. It's a cracked window finally shattering. I can't take it anymore.

I open my eyes to wide, startled brown ones staring back and then–

HANNA-MARIA VESTER

Secret Agents

                Suddenly, poems swoop in like domino
                    deities, one after the other.

                                          Andrea Gibson.

Mary Oliver.

                      Eileen Miles.

        The wind unleashes masterpiece after masterpiece.
They spread me out like dough, breathe

                              me into my body.

unstoppable

Like an   wave,

everywhere,

they are   ready to sneak into everything.

secret

Poems as   agents.

(Cue secret-agent-y tune:)

Couplets quadruple at the gym

as perfectly pronounced,

carefully piloted podcasts.

A comic soaks the audience

in light, in verse, and lifts me

into cosy armchaired night.

I witness the unexpected while I fall asleep

as sitcom characters

raise their rhymes.

Even when the swell   ing of my hip wanders
      to my chest,   I keep turning
        the burning spine.

           The words,   they bend
               genres   and me.
                  They   are
                       the   point

                make   body free

                they   are

           the   point

              the   point

                  is

                 me

                     they

        are

                           the

      poi

                                  nt

            .

HANNA-MARIA VESTER

In June of 2023, the editor considers all the people she has rejected over the years

I stand in the kitchen, reluctant
to chat with my flatmate, stomp
about the protest against CEAS[1], predictable,
preventable crime that steeps us in blood all over

again. Stunted, staccato,

I annotate books, put
'to withdraw (from sth)'
'to recoil'
'to flinch'
into vocabulary quizzes.
The milk boils softly, almost.

>   My brother called me last
>   Sunday. He seemed serious and

---

[1] That fucking European asylum programme, freshly streamlined. Makes it extremely difficult for people to reach safety. An agglomeration of "lawful" human rights violations. In June 2023.

in the midst of definition. On Saturday
my friends and I exhilarated
into drag, ate up gayness
as belongers, transformed into
free-breathers and lovers. We strutted,
but we may be props in AFD[2] propaganda

tomorrow. It's signified to be

> so young, so torn;
> steaming, stirring.

I annotate "resist" "repeat" "defy"
as 1933 goosesteps between our teeth
to grip the centric spine.

> We are free yet.
> I tell my brother, finally.

---

[2] That fucking German populist right-wing party, growing, electable and elected. A poster of theirs showed a bearded person in make-up preying on a child, a caricature of LGBTQ+ people reminiscent of Third Reich rhetoric. In June 2023.

DOROTHY LAWRENSON

The Highwayman

I was woken by the hall light going on and my mother entering the room. Lying still in the half-dark, hugging Big Teddy and staring at the wooden slats that supported the weight of my older brother Adam in the top bunk, I could hear muffled sounds—was he crying? The sheets ruffled. The bed frame creaked as he turned over. Then it steadied as Mum leant over his pillow and stroked his head, making soothing noises.

'I know, darling,' she said. 'It gets just as bad for Daddy sometimes.'

'It's not fair,' Adam sobbed. I pictured the red, raw skin of his forearms and lower legs. The itching was unbearable, but the urge to relieve it by scratching had to be resisted. That would only make the condition worse.

'When it gets bad,' Mum said, 'rub your skin with this towel. And then put on some more ointment.'

'It's just so unfair!'

I wondered if he was being bullied by the other boys in his class. To combat the dryness and itchiness of the eczema, he regularly had to slather himself with a dense, greasy petroleum jelly. He was as likely to attract attention for his oily-looking arms as for his scabbed and bleeding skin. The ointment's musty, medical smell pervaded the air of our bedroom, just as it soaked permanently into my brother's *Guardians of the Galaxy* duvet cover and my dad's shirt collars. My mum was never able to remove it fully by washing—but then, she was often more concerned with removing the bloodstains.

She was telling my brother this now, describing in surprising detail the occasions on which Dad had been hospitalised and treated with antibiotics or steroids because his cracked and broken skin could put up no barrier against infection. The details she described were unsettling, but her tone was soothing, almost hypnotic. On another occasion, she continued, Dad's condition mysteriously worsened until he again ended up in hospital, where the doctors discovered he had developed an allergy to the lanolin ointment he'd been prescribed—instead of soothing his skin, it inflamed it. Then there were the times, before modern inhalers, when an asthma attack had nearly killed him. At least Adam had only inherited his eczema and not its close companion, which tends to skip a generation.

My brother's breathing was quiet now, but Mum talked on. Her disembodied voice filled the semi-darkness—all I could see of her as she stood by the bed frame was a pair of legs in stout tweed trousers, a pair of feet in hand-embroidered slippers. It was like her to juxtapose the commonplace with the refined, to take the rough with the smooth. She was still talking about Dad, not about his skin anymore but about how hard he had been working that afternoon to replace the sash window on the stairs. Maybe, she suggested softly, Adam might help him to paint the frame tomorrow. Now she was describing her plans for the garden on which the window looked out—and with that, I knew Adam must be asleep. He wasn't interested in gardening.

I was in awe at Mum's skill. But at the same time, I basked in my astuteness at appreciating it—though not old enough to start school, in that moment, I felt worldly-wise. To coddle Adam, to praise his fortitude, or to utter platitudes—these would have enraged him. Instead, she subtly applied the balm of storytelling, to soothe him and transport him to another place, and eventually deliver him into sleep.

Two nights later, I too succumbed to Mum's art. I had been woken by a nightmare, or maybe just by the bitter east coast wind hurling rain against the windowpane. It was perhaps this wild weather that put Alfred Noyes' poem, 'The Highwayman', into Mum's mind. She perched herself on the edge of my bunk, smoothing my hair and tucking the duvet snugly under my chin. Then she took up the anthology and began to read:

The wind was a torrent of darkness among the gusty trees,
The moon was a ghostly galleon tossed upon cloudy seas,
The road was a ribbon of moonlight over the purple moor,
And the highwayman came riding—
Riding—riding—
The highwayman came riding, up to the old inn-door.

Before becoming a teacher, she had dabbled in amateur dramatics. I was captivated by her rhythmic, animated reading—I felt I was being carried away by the drumming hoofbeats of the highwayman's horse. When I reread the poem now, thirty-five years later, I can see why she used it in the classroom. It introduces many enchanting features of poetry, with its sparkling imagery of ribbon-like roads and jewelled skies, its onomatopoeia (*Over the cobbles he clattered and clanged in the dark inn-yard*), and its tragic love affair between the eponymous outlaw and Bess, the landlord's daughter.

Adam must have been asleep in the upper bunk. Or perhaps he too was lying with bated breath, as the redcoats lie in wait for the unwitting highwayman to ride into their trap. The lovers are betrayed by jealous Tim the ostler (*His eyes were hollows of madness, his hair like mouldy hay*), who tips off King George's men about their moonlight tryst at the inn. Bess is cruelly tied to the bed-post by the mocking soldiers, who ensure she can see, through the window, the road down which her doomed lover will ride:

They had tied her up to attention, with many a sniggering jest.
They had bound a musket beside her, with the muzzle beneath her breast!

In my memory (and as I reread the poem now), the narrative drives inexorably towards its thrilling conclusion, in which Bess takes the desperate action that alerts her lover to his danger—but I also know Mum must have frequently stopped *in medias res* to explain the vocabulary: what was an ostler? What was a casement? A musket? She told me about reading the poem to schoolchildren who sniggered at the word 'breast', which made me feel vastly mature for not doing so. In fact, the poem's sexual overtones were largely lost on me: the highwayman, with his skin-tight leather breeches and thigh-high boots, overpowered by Bess's loosened hair with its *black cascade of perfume…*

To the poem's original Edwardian readers, she must have seemed a role model, this dark-eyed, self-sacrificing romantic heroine, who unfurls her long, Rapunzel-like hair from the upstairs window as her lover rises upright in the stirrups to touch it. But my dark hair was cut short, just like Adam's, and I wore his hand-me-down corduroy trousers and checked shirts. I wanted to be the unnamed, dashing outlaw, with his French cocked-hat and coat of claret velvet, his rapier and his twinkling pistols.

All the same, Bess was the true protagonist of 'The Highwayman'. Though totally uninterested in princesses, I could get behind her sort of heroine. Not one who needed to be rescued, but one determined to save her gallant lover from a trap. Undeterred by the soldiers' mockery, she twists her hands behind her, struggling against the ropes for hours in the darkness, until finally she can touch the trigger:

The tip of one finger touched it; she strove no more for the rest!
Up, she stood up to attention, with the barrel beneath her breast—

How does this memory end? It must end in the blur of falling asleep to the imagined clatter of hooves in the old inn yard, merged with the real and ever-present east wind battering our sash windows and mingling with that stuffy smell of emulsifying ointment that pervades all my childhood memories. I'm sure I'm not alone in finding it difficult to pinpoint my earliest recollection. Anything amusing or unusual that happens in early childhood becomes a cute story, to be told and retold until the story is more memorable than the original experience. Like the occasion when my sister, dressed in a pure white knitted dress for some church event, went outside to find the deepest, muddiest puddle and calmly sat down in it, giggling. Or when I escaped from the garden and toddled down the road, barefoot, for half a mile. And then there was the time I nearly blinded Adam by stumbling against him with an unattended garden fork. But Mum lulling Adam to sleep with stories and introducing me to the comforting thrill of poetry—these are different. The reason I know they must be among my earliest memories is because I have never told them to anyone. These memories have escaped narrativization, until now. Paradoxically, they are ones in which storytelling is enshrined in memory. And yet, because they are about falling asleep, they also become vague and fade to black. Is it possible I could have drifted off before Bess heard the approaching hooves of the highwayman's horse in the frosty silence? Before she saw him coming down the ribbon of road, his face white in the moonlight? Before she pulled the trigger, *shattered her breast in the moonlight and warned him—with her death?* Since I know how it ends, how can this poem fail to eclipse my memory of first encountering it?

In a sense, what has happened with this poem is almost the opposite of the 'earliest-memory effect' I've just described. I've reread the poem so often since, but every time I do, I relive the experience of reading it for the first time, even though I know how it will end. Don Paterson writes that a poem is a machine for remembering itself, and that poetry is the only art form of which it can be said that remembering the work of art is the same thing as experiencing the work of art. (After all, when one remembers a novel, one remembers the plot and characters but not the exact form of the words.) Lying in the dark, seeing only in my mind's eye, I marvelled at the slippery, deceptive power of Mum's stories. Yet I had no such misgivings about the poem, which—defined by its very memorability, experienced as a memory and remembered as an experience—may constitute one of my earliest recollections.

MALINA SHAMSUDIN

The Huff Puff Hustle

I like my job – it's just mornings that don't spark joy. So, when a prospective client rocked up at 8.00 a.m. in desperate need of legal advice before catching a train, I was resentful. Overcompensated for professional guilt by offering him tea in my favourite mug. *May that pottery's cornflower glaze and curly hearts infuse sunshine in your morning, Sir.*

We're in a hole of an office within the bowels of Community Hall. I'm watching the client take a shaky sip from the wonky lip of said mug. The poor lighting throws bruises under his eyes and darkens his whiskery chin. His breathing is shallow, as if in short puffs. Bless his nervous soul.

'Mr Ham, there's really nothing to be worried about,' I say, placing his minted driver's licence on the corner of my dusty desk. I run my fingernail discreetly across the unblemished plastic for the bump of tactile engraving. *Hmm.*

The meeting is a formality to clarify the client's issue on record, so I may share the best legal aid options the Dark Forest community may provide. I hit the record button on my phone; my pen is poised over my notepad.

'Take a deep breath, and when you're ready, tell me again what brings you here today.'

NEW FILE: *Ham Vs. Brick Art Design Property Development ('B.A.D.')*

It's a predicament with a property developer, in triplicate. Like most first-time buyers, Mr Ham claims he had been so enchanted by the idea of owning a mortgage-free property in 12 short months, he didn't mind the cross-town move from Silver Linings; he had skimped on the necessary due diligence. Going for the smallest starter-home in full cash payment, he was dismayed to find the 'Cobb Deluxe' to be nothing more than a house of straw with weak walls that barely held up in a stiff wind.

(1) Breach of contract by B.A.D. Developer for failing to deliver a property that was safe and structurally sound.

Leaning into the two-year warranty, Mr Ham calls up the developer demanding reparation. The developer concedes – offering an upgrade to their two-bedroom 'Executive Log' model, in exchange for a non-disclosure agreement. Hardly believing his luck, Mr Ham jumps at the opportunity. After a spell in a grotty Airbnb, the log cabin is nothing more than a house of sticks that Mr Ham felt was unstable and prone to collapse.

(2) Misleading claims on B.A.D. Developer's expertise and assurances – possible coercion.

But then, the developer concedes the house lacks the quality and durability they had expected to deliver to Mr Ham and offers him a more established property as an alternative – the three-bedroom Stone Mansion – inclusive of temporary housing, removal costs, and waiving both council tax and utility bills for a year. Beguiled by their seemingly generous and compassionate offer, Mr Ham agreed. After another six-month wait, the much-anticipated home in brick-and-stone boasts a solid foundation, but deplorable finishings. As this isn't covered by the developer's warranty, and with no more funds to aesthetically do-up his first ever home, Mr Ham finds himself at a crossroad.

I underline Point (2). Mr Ham struggles with the oatmeal pockets of his trousers for an inhaler. He takes two deep puffs. As if in need of further fortification, he flings back the now tepid tea, flashing the familiar inscription at the swirly mug's base: 'Making things Just Right, Xmas 22 – Goldie Lak'. *Blast professionalism, I miss that mug.*

Mr Ham reaches into his pockets again to withdraw a fuchsia phone. Even upside down, I make out Mr Ham, and two others with such a striking resemblance they must be family. He taps onto a folder to share photographic evidence of his ordeal. The alleged houses of straw, sticks, and bricks.

Taking the phone, I zoom in for a closer inspection into the Stone Mansion's finishings: a portrait snap of a pristine kitchen with a well-worn island top, three neatly-stacked yet distinct swirly-hearted cornflower mugs, against a backdrop of built-in walnut cabinets; a landscape of what must be a living room with an undeniably rusty heater visible between a pastel armchair, a plaid rocking chair, and a pumpkin beanbag; a fish-lens shot of uneven but polished floorboards, in a space evidently capable of snugly fitting three beds. I also make out a beautiful silver frame with a familiar picture dotting each still. *Now we're cooking.*

A swoosh not unlike a toilet flush confirms digital copies have landed in my inbox. Mr Ham looks fried.

'What were you hoping legal aid would offer, Mr Ham?'

Mr Ham's chest folds as he blinks rapidly. In that moment, he is a plate of sadness, living on crumbs of hope and sanity.

'I want to burn that house to the ground,' he whispers. 'Fortunately, the property developer is willing to buy it back…and I just want to leave the Dark Forest. You can act as a conveyance solicitor, can you not?'

Mr Ham favours his inhaler with two more puffs.

He knows selling directly to a property developer potentially makes the whole process quicker and cheaper. No estate agents, no chain house sales. *But if we turned up the heat…*

'This depends on whether you really own the home, Mr Ham.'

Not a grunt nor a snuffle. It is I who leans forward, careful not to mince words.

'We must be wary of fraud – and here are the top three flags we solicitors look out for:

'*1 – Be wary of ID documents that have been issued recently.*'

I hand him his shiny driver's licence, tilting it on its axis. The too smooth plastic displays a hologramme, but the optically variable ink struggles in a solitary green.

'*2 – The seller has little knowledge of the property they are selling.*'

I turn my monitor screen to showcase the picture of the bedroom from Mr Ham's phone. 'It's a bit difficult to imagine the need for three beds crammed into a single room, when you've been upgraded into a three-bedroom home.'

'*3 – It's a high value property with no mortgage, requiring a quick sale.*'

Clearly, he has sound reasons on this point. 'Mr Ham – it is rare indeed for anyone to have the same photo – in triplicate, in each room, no matter how beautiful the picture frame.' I show him the familiar snapshot of him and his two look-alikes that grace both his home screen and each evidence photo. 'Why do you?'

A plasticky clunk as the inhaler hits the herringbone floor.

'This is just too close to the "Stealing Your Home" hustle, Mr Ham. It's usually the conveyancing solicitor that is not located close to the property, but in this case, the home in question looks surprisingly like the one-bedroom owned by the Bears. They host fabulous Murder Mystery soirées, so I'm quite familiar with their home.'

That chinny chin chin quivers.

'It's a property developer's cookie cutter design. All houses look the same,' says Mr Ham, crisping with a shortening temper.

'Yes, but it's the unique touches that seem to give it away.'

I pull up the picture of the kitchen, zooming into the crockery.

'Where did you get those mugs, Mr Ham?'

'H&M Home tat,' comes with an edge.

'You would have had better luck citing a charity shop. Unfortunately, they are a limited-edition Christmas gift from the town matchmaker to a select group of friends. One of which you're drinking from.'

'We don't live under bridges here, Sir.'

The Dark Forest Civil Legal Aid aren't the trolls he was looking for. As Mr Ham tersely excuses himself to catch a train, I can't help the odd crackling of injustice sprinkled with awe. *Doesn't audacity mark the chops of a true thespian?* I email him an application to the Actors Guild of Dark Forest, attaching an audition flyer for the next community theatre.

Yes, I like my job. And a good mug always sparks joy.

DAVID BLAKESLEE

Generation

On the eve of his thirty-eighth birthday, while taking out the recycling, the man realized the box he was carrying was the exact shape of his childhood home. It was not a strange shape, a rectangle like most other boxes, but as he stood in the driveway, a light rain splattering the top of his balding head, he saw that the four sides of the box were the exact proper dimensions to match the outer walls of the house he was raised in. And as he stepped towards the bin, he imagined where the door would be, the front window, the kitchen. What had once been his whole world was now resting between his hands in miniature.

He stayed up late that night. Using his memory and a few old photographs, he marked the floorplan of the interior walls with a number two pencil and then hid the box in his closet. Over the next few days, in spare minutes away from his wife and five-year-old son, he made minor additions to the model. He cut and folded an envelope until it resembled the general shape of the threadbare living room couch, transformed a bottle cap into the table where Chelsea fell and knocked out her front teeth. Little by little, the details emerged as he tried to account for every piece of furniture in the home, placing them all exactly where he remembered them being.

The little house consumed his thoughts. In meetings he daydreamed, wrestled over details: Did Mom put the magazine rack to the right or the left of the television? Was the rocking chair facing towards the window or away from it? He scribbled floor plans in the margins of inter-office mail. He found a listing for the house online, one that had been posted years before it was demolished, and clicked through the photos of every room.

He remembered small things he hadn't thought about in years. When he cut toothpicks to build the bunk bed, he remembered how Dad had built it out of two used bed frames, how he used a hacksaw to shorten the legs before stacking them, and how Chelsea would tap out coded messages on the bottom of his mattress in the middle of the night when it was so late they knew they would get in trouble for talking.

When he added the detail of the kitchen floor, he remembered where Mom had dropped a pizza box after absentmindedly setting it on top of the hot stove, and how the burning cardboard had left a black scorch mark on the linoleum that was impossible to scrub out.

He did this all in secret. He would crawl out of bed, creep past his son's room, turn on one lamp by the dining room table, and continue the construction in total silence. The only sounds in the whole world were the slicing of scissors through sheets of paper, the slow creaking tear of a piece of tape leaving its dispenser, and the occasional clatter of paper clips and thumbtacks falling to the floor. His wife either slept through it all or chose not to question what he was doing out of bed in the middle of the night. He worried she would disapprove somehow. He didn't know why, but he knew he had to be the only one attending to the model. He knew that as soon as someone else touched it, it would be ruined forever.

Eventually, the furniture was set, but the empty little house felt lonely, so the man found little trinkets to stand in for the family. For Dad, he pilfered a green plastic soldier from his son's toy box. For Chelsea, he found a stick of fruity sugar-free gum. For Mom, he nabbed an empty pill bottle from the back of the medicine cabinet. For himself, he repurposed a little metal figurine of a dog from a board game that was collecting dust in the hall closet. He moved these tokens around the little cardboard house according to his memories, reenacting every fragment of his childhood that was still in his brain.

Nightly, he pulled out the box and used it as a portal to another world, rode it deep into his own past, and saw the figures come alive. He moved them with intricate precision. The plastic soldier had a solid gait, the stick of gum was bouncy, the pill bottle was frantically all places at once, and the dog was fast and carefree. His favorite nights were the nights when all the pieces ended up together in the same room, usually toppled over onto the paper-envelope couch in front of the matchbox TV. But then the soldier would get up and leave, or the gum and the dog would start fighting, and the pill bottle would storm off in frustration.

Months later, he sat down with the figures and realized he had nothing left to remember. He had reenacted his entire childhood, and there would be no more nights in the little house. It came time for Chelsea to meet Bill, time for him to go off to college. He knew soon Dad would have his accident, and Mom would get sick. He held the figures in his hands, and they were so light, so small, so impermanent. It was finally time to recycle the box and be done with it. But as he took a step toward the door, he heard a tiny voice squeak out of his own hand.

"What's wrong honey? You look blue."

He looked down at the pill bottle. He must be imagining things.

"It's always the same with him," the soldier responded, wrestling his way out from behind a finger. "He takes it all oo personally."

"He's sensitive!" the bottle rattled, her voice catching in her throat.

"You see what you've done? Now she's upset! Why do you always do this?" the soldier shouted.

"Dad, can't you just give it a rest for once?" the stick of gum snapped. She folded herself away from the other items into his open palm. Then, lowering her voice, "But this is actually really weird. Even for you. You should, like, see a doctor or something."

"All he needs is to grow up! Get his head on straight, stop playing with toys."

He set the box on the ground and put the figurines inside, sitting down cross-legged to get a closer look. The soldier wobbled over to the tin dog, who was now cowering in the corner. He pointed the tip of his plastic rifle at the animal. "This is what you think of yourself? You think you're just a little pup? For God's sake, show some backbone."

The pill bottle rolled over and placed herself between the soldier and the dog. "He's sweet and kind and trusting. Are those such bad qualities?"

The stick of gum flipped end over end up to the drawing of the kitchen window. "It never stops with you two! Why did you insist on putting us through this? No wonder he turned out how he did. No offense."

The dog rocked side to side on its stiff, diecast legs. There was a sound coming from somewhere inside, but it couldn't speak. It just whined and moaned, like someone screaming underwater, muffled beyond comprehension.

"You're weak!" said the soldier.

"You're just misguided, a little lost," argued the pill bottle.

"Isn't there a door in this thing?" the gum wondered, already planning her escape.

Just then, another voice, clearer, from behind him. "Dad? What are you doing?"

His son, hair slicked sideways from sleep, pajamas wrinkled, finger in nose.

He looked back to the box and the figures all sat silently, once more inanimate.

The little boy walked over, squatted down. "Are you playing with this?" He examined the model house, ran his chubby fingers along the floors, gazed through the roof like a giant peering out of heaven.

Without giving time for a response, the little boy promptly picked up the figures and began to move them around the tiny rooms, tossing them against the walls, slamming them into each other, racing them around, smashing them through the makeshift furniture. Then he took the pill bottle, cracked it open, put the soldier and the stick of gum inside it, and shook it around like a maraca, giggling all the while. The figures remained silent but the man could imagine the sound of their screams. Eventually, the boy got bored and tossed it down. Then he picked up the little dog. "I like it," he said, "bark bark."

A light flipped on overhead, and the man's wife appeared around the corner. "I thought I heard voices here. What on earth is happening?" She looked to both the man and the boy for answers.

"Dad was playing with this."

She rolled her eyes. "Everyone get back to bed." She took his son by the hand and started to lead him down the hall. She called behind her, "Babe, please remember to take out the recycling in the morning."

NICOLE CHRISTINE CARATAS

Last Lie

She lied to me as I hauled up the anchor. The wind didn't blow, and the seabirds kept their beaks shut.

'It's so nice to reconnect,' she said. It wasn't her first lie, but if Lady Luck was on my side, it would be her last.

'You look lovely in that frock.'

Okay, *that* would be her last lie.

She sat on the bow as I steered us out into the centre of the loch. The tourists hadn't flocked to the Highlands yet. With the exception of a few stray hikers – keen wannabe outdoorsmen who couldn't handle hiking real mountains – we were alone.

Fifteen years of friendship. We'd been inseparable once.

We used to take our Barbies out to the woods, climbing trees with our matching dolls tucked into the waistbands of our skirts. We'd race as high as our little limbs could carry us. I'd let her win sometimes, to make sure she was happy.

I brought the boat to a stop. When I pulled in the throttle, I felt a twinge in my elbow. Once during our races, I fell out of a tree. Landed with my Barbie's face in my elbow, and it hasn't been right since. She always thought I was faking the pain.

We bobbed on the loch. Waves of my own making gently rocked us until the water stilled.

'Join me up here,' she said. I sat on the bench opposite her, slipping my sun hat down to block the glare off the water.

She swivelled in her seat, the toes she painted green skimming the boat floor. Then, she leaned forward and reached her hands towards me, palms up. Her eyes urged me to put my hands in hers, and though a part of me wanted to recoil, I did it.

When we were teenagers, we'd hold hands over a Ouija board. She always wanted to summon her ancestors, boring old dead people who didn't matter because she'd never met them. I thought we should reach out to Elvis or Princess Di. Someone who could tell us a famous secret that we could publish in a best-selling biography or make into a movie. She never was pragmatic like me, only thinking of herself.

The boat swayed gently. A cool spring day, enough rain in the forecast that the loch would be murky, but we were still dry.

'I'm sorry for everything,' she lied again. 'I know I'm not a very good friend. Or, I should say, I know I haven't been. But that will all change now. I'm here for good. You can count on me!'

It was worse than when she borrowed my collection of Edgar Allan Poe stories, swearing she'd take care of it, and returned it all dog-eared and coffee-stained. 'It was like that when you gave it to me!' she had insisted, as if I would ever treat a book like that.

The lies never stopped. One after another; I would have been impressed had they not been at my expense.

She squeezed my hands once, twice, then waited for me to do the same. I smiled and returned the gesture. Out in the middle of the loch, with no one around, I wasn't about to let her think something was wrong.

We were twenty when she lashed out. Not at me, not at first. Some loser in a club swore she had ghosted him. She claimed she didn't recognise him, but he wrapped a meaty hand around her arm and tried to pull her away from me. I smacked him across the face, but when he let go and stormed out of the club, it was *me* she was angry with. It was *me* she raged at. It was *me* she abandoned on the sticky dance floor.

She called me three days later. 'I was drunk,' she cried. 'And you were being a bitch, but you were being a bitch for me, and that's really nice.'

I guess it wasn't really an apology, but I forgave her anyway. Like I always do.

Did.

Life went on, and we found ourselves living in different cities. I tried to maintain the friendship. I called her all the time. I even went to visit her, bought tickets for the same festival she had plans to attend. But when the weekend of the festival came around, she told me not to come. 'There will be too many people from work,' she lamented. 'I'll be so busy entertaining them that I just won't be any fun to be around.' I told her I didn't mind. I could mingle with her colleagues – it wasn't like I needed a babysitter. 'I'm just too stressed,' she insisted. 'I'll pay you back for your ticket!'

So I drove the six hours home. She never did pay me back. Then she was suddenly very hard to contact. Emails left unanswered, calls unreturned. Birthdays passed without a bloody text message.

It took her years, actual years to reach out. To 'reconnect' as she put it. I had moved on – I knew my worth. But she just couldn't go on without me.

'Help me!' she shouted from the loch. It happened so fast, I don't even know what went down besides *her*. One minute she was sitting across from me, yelling something I couldn't quite make out, and the next, she was in the water, flailing like a Magikarp. 'I can't swim!'

I flung the life preserver.

I haven't been able to throw straight since I fell out of that tree.

The wind picked up the life preserver and blew it across the loch, away from us.

The boat started drifting, further and further from where she struggled to stay afloat. As I started the engine, the words she'd yelled floated back to me, her last lie.

'I'm your best friend!'

I advanced the throttle as the sun dipped below the Munro, and I knew she could never lie to me again.

GERRY STEWART

Night Turnings
After A Scots Quair

Sunset fires the birch trees to amber,
whispering to their roots.
She waits for the glow
to touch her skin,
untethering her.

When she lets go
in the gloaming,
she becomes you
in the gloaming.

You, that other girl,
a twin-soul coiled
behind her breastbone,
fluttering like hope.

You're not held
in the years' tight grip.
You can leave the house
where light escapes
like a dying breath.

Run to the hills,
wind-tangled hair, eyes stinging,
take on the whirl
of both love and loss.
Know you will never return

to grow old
within that house.

You burn with the trees,
the embrace of sky and flame,
not caring if the road back
will always be there.

Dance to the stars rising
above ancient earth and stones.
This is your song –
it will never abandon you.

She wakes in her room
to the scratch of dishes,
the children's voices clattering
until night comes to close the curtains.

GERRY STEWART

Pentecost

After the painting by Andrew Wyeth

She sees the landscape I offer as stark,
dreary in mud and tempura.
I see gold,
the wind lifting my spirit
like the lace of salt-riddled nets.

Yet I view her winter
with an Atlantic hate,
my solid coast swept away
by the ghost of my drowning
while she adapts,
firm-rooted to native.

And though I don't believe
my nature is torn and ratted
or hers protected-safe,
I recognise the breath
that pins us
in the same place
as divine.

GERRY STEWART

Evening River Swim at Ansku Sauna

The cool water against my thighs
is a welcome shock
after a long hot day.

I tread the sand
hesitation
before taking a breath
and dropping down
weighted.

Burst the surface
I am slick
rinsed clean
in silken water.

I float head back
suspended in clear amber.

Deaf to all the noise
I carried with me
emptied
of the worries
that push me under
my eyes fill with the soft blue
fringed by birch.

Evening River Swim at Anksu Sauna / 55

Swallows arrow
wings sun-tipped
through the thick summer air

              away
      away
away.

EMERSON ROSE CRAIG

Resume

Elise Beyer
Personal Assistant

Elise Beyer has worked as a personal assistant for ~~the last four hundred years~~ fifteen years. She is devoted to organization and has extensive experience in event scheduling, office tidying, ~~speaking dead languages~~, research, budgeting, editing, ~~medieval combat, mediating between opposing royal factions, and stopping world-ending events on a regular basis!~~

I deleted another sentence. Working on a resume was always a painful process, but I hadn't even considered how hard it would be when I wasn't supposed to tell anyone what my current job entailed. It wasn't just the NDAs I had signed; when saving the world was part of your job description, you started taking consequences very seriously.

It wasn't that I hated my job: there were many travel opportunities, I was able to attend once-in-a-lifetime events and even take part in them, and my boss was the sweetest person (if a bit scatterbrained). But who wouldn't be if they spent their whole lifetime jumping around from one time period to the next, always witnessing the world out of chronological order? That, of course, was the root of the problem.

Education:
BA in Business, Carleton University, September 2004 to June 2008.

Work Experience:
Personal Assistant to Jessie Smith, July 2008 to Present.
Barista, Coffee Lovers, September 2004 to July 2008.

After fifteen years of my life and witnessing countless decades at this job, I was starting to lose myself. I had lost months when the Time Traveler hadn't brought me back to the same moment I had left. Family and friends simply accepted that I would sometimes disappear for work. I had missed birthdays, weddings, and funerals. It had been over five years since I had been on a date because I kept missing dinner reservations. And the dalliances with long-dead knights and sailors didn't count, did they? My neighbor even stole my cat – not that I could actually be mad about that, someone needed to take care of *Meow Antoinette*. The people I loved were moving on without me. There had been one night where I had gotten home well after dark and fumbled blindly at the wall searching for the light switch when my feet slipped out from under me. When I finally flipped the switch, I realized I was sitting on a large pile of mail. As I sifted through bills and magazines, a smiling baby looked up at me. It was a birth announcement from my best friend from college. As I looked through the pile, I also found the pregnancy announcement and an invitation to the baby shower. When I called to congratulate her, she told me she had wanted to make me godmother, but... she didn't need to finish the sentence for me to understand. I was no longer around.

I'd taken the job right out of college when I was in desperate need of a better-paying position than that of barista to tackle my student debt. It sounded so perfect then, like I was a character in a book setting out on a great adventure. The Time Traveler had been a regular at the coffee shop for a few weeks, showing up every day with a different oversized knit cardigan (somehow, they were always cold) and their red curls drooping over their dark eyes. When I saw them put up a flier for a personal assistant, I jumped at the chance. They were always kind and tipped well, and the job promised travel. We talked for hours after my shift, discussing everything from our favorite books to political opinions to the merits of pineapple on pizza. I then underwent an extensive background check and signed my name on a large stack of legal documents. At first, I assumed this strange person must be a celebrity; of course, the reality was much more exciting... and dangerous.

Skills:
- Research
- ~~Latin~~
- Problem Solving
- Adaptability
- ~~Medieval Hebrew~~
- Negotiation
- ~~Pictish~~
- ~~Sword Fighting~~
- Teamwork
- ~~Viking Farming~~
- ~~Embroidery~~
- Time Management

What kind of skills were appropriate to put on a resume anyway? And if questioned, how would I begin to explain how I learned half of these skills? Would people believe I had just casually learned Medieval Hebrew? Perhaps I could forge a dead private tutor. Or perhaps I should do online school and gain some degrees to justify my knowledge. That could open up some opportunities to work at a university or museum as a researcher. But did I even want to work as a researcher? Studying events I'd already witnessed and arguing with people about what actually happened – when I didn't have proof – didn't sound all that fun. Perhaps I could write a book instead. Reveal enticing tales of the affairs and murders I had observed. I could write a whole series on my few meetings with Julie d'Aubigny. I bit my lip, thinking of the last knight to tell me he loved me, only to die in battle days later. No, the point of leaving this job was to start living in the present. Anything to do with history was out. Skills be damned. It was just a shame that my boss had never needed me to do any social media management. It was a real hole in my resume for any job I might want to get in this century.

I glanced through what I had written so far. I placed my cursor in the one spot that I had left completely blank.

Career Goals:

A friend told me that I should have a career goal statement at the top, something to tie together the strange pieces of my resume and give potential employers an idea of what I was striving for.

If I had been asked this question before I started working as the Time Traveler's assistant, I could have spurted plenty of answers. Help create change. See the world. Work with and create a collaborative community with creative individuals. But I had already accomplished all of these things. Quick internet searches didn't help, either. They only asked me questions about where I saw myself in five years. My mind was blank. What did the future hold for me? What did I want from it? In my years with the Time Traveler, career-focused goals became meaningless compared with genuine connection. What did I want out of my future? To not know how my friends were going to die. To keep promises to my loved ones.

I resisted the urge to smash all the keys down at once and see if a coherent sentence would magically appear. This wasn't even going to be the hardest part. I hadn't told the Time Traveler that I was quitting. They couldn't function without an assistant, since they lived life out of order and were generally bad at organization. It was hard for them when the assistants left. When I had started, I thought I was going to be different. Why quit when you had a boss who was thoughtful, genuine, and supportive? Naively, I believed I could spare the Time Traveler the pain of my goodbye. But time had worn me down, just like each assistant before me. I cleared my throat, trying not to cry. It wasn't like I would never see them again. They were the Time Traveler, after all. And I would stay on to help them hire and train the next assistant. It would be fine.

The Time Traveler crashed into the room, knocking over a large stack of books. "Elise, we have to get going. Start the engine. Where are my keys?" Their eyes were wide as they patted themselves down.

I sighed and tried to suppress the smile tugging at my lips. "The keys are on your belt. I thought you were getting lunch in Constantinople. What happened?"

I closed my laptop and hurried to get the time machine ready for departure. There would be time to work on my resume later.

ANTHI CHEIMARIOU

Blind World
for the "Blind Film Critic"

Words like *transparent, translucent,* and *opaque*
do not exist. No one can see beyond things,

nor into them. "How are Ice cubes the same colour
as the sea? How do doorknobs reflect colours?"[1]

Reflection of light means nothing to you: blank dreams,
no images or people; no judgement or fear.

Vivid dreams full of laughter and music.
What if the world was not blind?

Terracotta dresser when you open your eyes,
flickering brown eyes to your left. A medley

of colours in the brick of day, a window that reveals
the world beyond the naked orange bodies.

You know them as orange through the vibrations
of their bodies, something you as a blind man can see.

Maybe if the world were blind, it could see
through the window its own shadowy perception

beyond the cave, where colours become
sounds, and things become transparent.

[1] Quotation from the famous "Blind Film Critic"

ANTHI CHEIMARIOU

Words

a white dove, no this is too evocative,
a black raven, no this is too obtuse,
a grey elephant, no this is too real,
a silver strand of hair, no this is the future,
a beautiful comma, no this is a breath,
a lonely colon, no this is a full stop.

Who gives the senses an idea of freedom?

A mind palace without familiar places
faces, only colours –

this is you.

ANTHI CHEIMARIOU

Amygdala Hijack[1] – Oxytocin:

a chemical in the brain that is responsible for social bonding, hate, and, more specifically, a mother's love

The taste of mud
and five fingerprints
on her cheek

teeth blackened
quivering limbs
preparing to pounce

a constricted throat
a second without
sound, tightened jaw

and goosebumps
dominate her body,
prefrontal cortex

closed, so she sees only
one perspective: you with
the orange blouse; *you*

are wrong and we're
going to fight
she forgets the sunrise

and the forging lilies
she only sees a threat
and she is ready to die.

Echoes from memories
lost. For her – she is
protecting her child,

but in the eye of the
beholder, she is the one
in the muddied red dress.

[1] https://hbr.org/2015/12/calming-your-brain-during-conflict

KATIE HAY-MOLOPO

The Art of Delivery

Certain people have said that, when attending to someone in a stressful situation, it is most helpful to remain calm, especially when additional stressors arise. For instance, if you ever find yourself singing soprano as part of the National Choir for the President's inauguration and you notice halfway through the third verse of the National Anthem that there's a rare stinging ant crawling across the collared robe of the baritone standing in the row in front of you, it is best that you simply fake a quiet sneeze and gently blow the ant onto the floor so you can silently crush it under your shoe. This is far preferable to smacking at it with your flimsy choir book in a panic, because these sorts of ants are prone to stinging when startled and baritones are prone to screaming when stung, and no one wants to be remembered as the one who censored the nation's theme song with a bellow, even if it is guaranteed to be in key.

One way to remain calm in stressful situations is to have a plan in place. Thinking once more about your unfortunate stinging ant incident, you're far more likely to keep a level head if you know ahead of time that the venue will be outdoors and so you will have researched the meteorological tendencies of the area as well as its flora and fauna. In doing so, you'll have found that in that part of the country at that particular time of year, stinging ants are abundant because of the genus of grass with which presidential types insist on seeding their lawns. And since you'll have done your research and know these ants are wingless and it takes them a good 3.7 seconds to realize they're in danger, the prospect of calmly knocking the insect to the ground to meet its demise won't seem so far-fetched after all. In fact, considering the circumstances, your actions make perfect sense, and, overall, there will be absolutely no cause for alarm.

This is how I imagine my labor and delivery team started their night, feeling cool as cucumbers, a phrase which has nothing to do with the salad you had for lunch and instead means, "well-prepared, relaxed, and ready to deliver as many babies as are determined to exit the womb." After all, medical professionals are masters of what are called contingency plans—the Plan Bs and 2.0s and just-in-cases—which is why I wouldn't at all be surprised to find my labor nurses had a doppler on hand in case the fetal heart monitor belt popped a seam, or that they had already alerted the on-call obstetrician by the time we'd arrived because my doctor lived a good half hour away and she needed extra time to extract clean scrubs from the nethermost regions of her closet. These and more wouldn't surprise me at all, which is probably why I was so surprised—and yes, I'll admit, even amused—when we rolled up to the maternity center and within fourteen minutes, it was as if all calm had flown out the window and everyone's cucumber-like state had absolutely deteriorated.

My husband tells me it was quite the scene. I wouldn't know; I hadn't opened my eyes since I'd climbed onto the bed in the triage room, completely ignored my nurses' instructions to lay on my back so they could check my dilation, and started pushing. But my husband tells me that by the time they'd trundled me from the prep room into the room where we'd be staying, there were five nurses standing around me, each of them trying to be well-prepared, relaxed, and ready to deliver the baby according to the plan that was falling apart before their very eyes. One nurse held the fetal monitoring belt, probably regretting asking if I wanted it wrapped around my belly. Another held a bag of fluids and a drip line, the Pitocin that I didn't want or need but that they had to give. There was a nurse holding paperwork, including the consent forms I hadn't yet signed giving the hospital staff permission to do all the things they had insofar been unsuccessful in doing.

And there must have been more things left in more hands, as there were five nurses anxious to perform their obligatory duties and I've only specified three, but then my waters broke and the baby's head popped out and suddenly—and this is the part I remember as vividly as you might remember a bellowing baritone interrupting the National Anthem because of a wingless stinging ant, a flimsy choir book, and an ill-prepared soprano—suddenly the room erupted with shouting.

"PUSH!"

"KEEP PUSHING!"

The Art of Delivery / 69

"TIME TO GET ON YOUR BACK MAMA ROLL OVER!"

"DON'T BREATHE JUST HOLD YOUR BREATH BEAR DOWN AND *PUSH*!"

"THE HEAD'S BEEN OUT FOR A MINUTE YOU NEED TO PUSH *NOW* MAMA!"

Now, let's be clear about something: professional medical advice is generally very helpful and not something you should ignore. For instance, if you love skateboarding but happen to live in a neighborhood peppered with hills and poison ivy, it makes sense to heed your doctor's admonition to wear a beekeeper's suit in addition to your standard helmet and elbow pads while ollieing in front of Mrs. Jacobs' house so you don't end up in the hospital covered in scrapes and hives again. Or if you're allergic to shellfish, it makes sense to submit to your doctor's vehement protest against entering the county's inaugural shrimp-eating contest, even if your mother is the one organizing the event and it will be held in your backyard and your crush will be attending. Indeed, in light of that last bit of information, listening to your doctor makes even more sense because holding hands in the back of an ambulance with your crush only happens to people like my cousin Jeff, while you're likely to end up simply leaving the party with a swollen face and a big bill for anaphylactic shock.

Clearly, you should listen to your doctor—just as clearly as this statement is about to be refuted using "unless". Listen to your doctor—unless you're giving birth and it's clear that the commands ricocheting around the room are contrary to the commands pulsating through your body.

"Relax."

"Breathe deeply."

"Take this moment to be still. Let everything settle."

"You are safe. The baby is safe. You're almost there. Keep going, Mama."

"We're not out of this yet, but we're so close. Be ready and let it happen. She's almost here."

My husband tells me that when the panicked commands started, he wanted to tell everyone to "Shut up!"—strong language from a man who knows all the words to the Mickey Mouse Funhouse "Stretch Break" song. But then he saw that my face was perfectly calm and so he kept quiet because he knew that while pointedly ignoring every shred of professional medical advice hurled at me was doing nothing to soothe the nerves of my attending nurses, it was doing wonders to facilitate the healthy and safe delivery of our baby, and, at the end of the day, that was what was most important.

"At the end of the day" is a funny phrase, not because it is humorous but because the "end" of this "day" was technically the very beginning of many things, including that day which was a Tuesday. It was the beginning of our daughter's life outside the womb, a time in which she has already experienced a hurricane, being poked with a purple crayon, and the unfortunate midnight insomnia brought on by too much caffeine. It was also the beginning of maternity leave and the notorious fourth trimester, a time set aside for bingeing *The Chosen* and *Young Sheldon*, moonlighting as a milk machine, and taking entire afternoons to cook and consume ten pounds of sesame chicken. And it was the beginning of the telling and retelling of this same story, over and over and in as many forms as we can contrive, knowing that the details vary depending on who's doing the telling and listening and that while the significance of certain moments changes as life continues to be lived, the heart of the story always remains the same.

For at the end of the day—no matter how explosive the entrance, how divergent the process, how frightening the quiet breaths in between—every one of us should do our best to remain cool as cucumbers because every story begins in the midst of another already ongoing, and there is simultaneously very little and everything in the world to be done about that.

MIRIAM HUXLEY

Tsk, Tsk

There were sunflowers in a vase on the table, placed just off-centre. It was an old vase – cut glass, their mother would've said – and not quite the right thing for such top-heavy flowers. Mum wouldn't have liked the sunflowers at all. *Garish.* A roll of the eyes. *Tsk.* The familiar sound of disappointment. *Tsk. Too bright.*

Who are you trying to fool?

Bee moved the vase to the left. She stood back, one hand on the chair, admiring the intense yellow-orange, the spiky seeds, the pointed leaves curling away from the brown faces.

Tam always loved sunflowers. She said they reminded her of their childhood, when they spent long summer days in the garden playing make-believe. They never had sunflowers in their garden, but the neighbours did, and each year, the plants would grow so tall that the bright petals waved over the top of the fence, like friends the girls were always waiting for.

But that was a long time ago, and Bee didn't know what Tam thought about anything anymore.

She pushed the thought out of her mind and returned to tidying, straightening picture frames, rearranging the knick-knacks on the mantle, dusting the clock even though it had been broken for some time now. She looked at her watch, then pushed the gold, broken hands until they both sat close to the twelve.

It wouldn't be long now.

•

Gravel crunched underfoot as Tam walked down the still yet-to-be paved (never-to-be paved) path leading to the house she'd left twenty years earlier. She stopped, dropping her heavy bag with a thud, and stood looking at the place she had hoped she'd never come back to. As predicted, it looked the same. Or maybe the same but worse, blue paint peeling, wooden window frames rotting, a moss-covered roof, and tree branches drooping perilously close to the building. One storm, that's all it would take to send one of the cedars right through the house. She'd expected this. Bee didn't know how to take care of things. At least, not anything beyond the front door.

Tam picked her bag up and continued crunching up the never-going-to-happen unpaved driveway.

•

Bee always thought she'd hear from Tam sooner.

But it had been twenty years of almost nothing. The occasional phone call to celebrate a holiday or a birthday. Tam never left a phone number, or an address. Sometimes she sent postcards with brightly coloured pictures of exotic locations like Greece or Bali. Bee kept them tucked away in an old shoebox in her closet. When they arrived through the letterbox, Mum told Bee to throw them away. When Bee refused, Mum came back with the eye roll. *Tsk*.

When Mum died, Bee filled in the details for the death

notice with emotionless care, trying to imbue each of the allowed words with a message for Tam. *She is survived by* actually meant *come home*. But the funeral passed without word from Tam, and then months passed, and then another year passed.

Bee was surprised.

No, she was more than surprised. She was distraught, finally admitting that she had been left alone in a house she hated, living a life she hadn't wanted, and now she was wrong for assuming that she knew her sister after all these years.

That was when it happened.

She was in the kitchen, heating up a tin of cream of mushroom soup. There was a sound, and it wasn't the clank of the wooden spoon against the metal pot, or the rush of gas through the element, it was something more familiar. It was a sound engrained in her mind.

She continued stirring until she heard it again. She turned around, holding the spoon above her head like a weapon.

What do you think you're doing with that? Going to stir me to death? Too late.

There was no doubt in Bee's mind that Mum was standing on the other side of the kitchen, laughing at her. She was dressed in her purple fluffy housecoat, her grey hair wrapped tight in pink plastic curlers. She was just as Bee had found her two years earlier, except that she was surrounded by a faint glimmer. You could almost call it a sparkle.

Bee dropped the spoon.

Now look what you've done, silly girl. The voice sounded exactly as it had when Mum was alive.

Silly girl, always silly girl, even when Bee's hair

started to grey, and she no longer recognised herself in the mirror.

•

Tam couldn't remember exactly where she was when Mum's ghost showed up in a fluffy purple housecoat, her hair in pink curlers. It might have been when she was lodging in that Victorian mansion in Edinburgh, or maybe when she spent a summer on a sheep farm in County Clare. Either way, the ghost arrived and refused to leave, no matter how many times Tam said she wasn't interested in being haunted. The ghost was unmoved by Tam's statement that she didn't believe in ghosts.

That's not any way to talk to your mother.

'How do I even know you're my mother? I haven't seen you in years,' Tam responded.

But she knew the sparkly ghost was her mother – they had the same turned-up noses, the same nostrils that flared out when they spoke. And, if she'd needed further confirmation, the ghost had looked around the dusty old room in Edinburgh, or the cramped attic in Ireland, and said, *Is this where you live now?*

And then Tam heard that familiar sound. *Tsk.*

•

The *tsk, tsk* was as constant as the ticking of the clock on the mantle.

For years, that was the sound Bee heard every time she did something wrong. Even when she thought she'd done something thoughtful, or considerate, like bringing a bouquet in from the garden to brighten up the kitchen.

Silly girl, who do you think you're convincing with those flowers?

Or if Bee closed the heavy drapes on days when the wind howled, and the cold rattled the windows.

Silly girl, now I can't see the view. What's the point in all this, the shimmering finger pointed out at the ocean, the tree-covered islands in the inlet, the place where they sometimes saw dolphins and whales, *if you're just going to cover it up?* And then the ghost tried to pull the drapes open, but her fingers went right through the fabric.

That was why Bee did it.

Broke the clock, that is.

On a cold morning, when it was still dark and the windows had a layer of ice on the inside, she wound the hands the wrong way until she heard the crunching and grinding of gears.

'It just stopped working,' she'd explained with a shrug, 'I could try to get it fixed, but I'm sure it will be expensive.'

That was an heirloom! Silly girl.

•

Tam expected some kind of response from her mother's ghost when she brought her home. Maybe a hallelujah chorus and a beam of light to take her away.

Instead, the ghost shook her head.

Silly girl's let this place go to ruin.

That was when Tam dropped her bag on the ground. The thud was meant to be emphatic.

But the ghost carried on.

All those years I looked after this place, and you and your sister, and this is how you repay me?

Tam pushed her hair – bleached after a summer spent in the desert sun – off her forehead and the ghost's words from her mind. She had spent so many years not thinking about her mother. And now here she was, back home again, with her mother standing-but-not-standing next to her.

So she reminded the ghost, 'I'm here to see Bee.'

•

Bee answered the door at the first knock.

'It's you!' Bee said, wondering why she sounded surprised. She looked into her sister's face, once a mirror image, and noticed lines in different places, the skin tanned a few shades darker, and the hair, golden at the ends.

Tam walked into the house. She started to look around. Then she walked right through their mother's ghost.

•

Tam wasn't surprised that nothing had changed. Well, something had changed. When Bee opened the door, Tam had studied her sister, wondering if she would've looked the same if she'd been the one who stayed. But she'd spent a lifetime telling herself that she didn't need to feel guilty. She'd told her mother's ghost that she didn't feel guilty. And now she was home, for her sister. She stopped at the back of the house, standing right at the midpoint of the wall of windows. The view hadn't changed either, and it was still so beautiful that it made her want to cry.

•

When they spotted the pod of orcas down in the inlet, Bee realised it was just the two of them in comfortable silence, just her and Tam standing at the window.

THOMAS CARROLL

Boat///House

It was dark by the time that work was done. The air still and the sky heavy, as if it might finally snow. There had been no warning of anything on the daily program, but still it was best to make towards home. He offered the usual farewells and started on his way, cutting down across the frostbitten park and through the street that led onto his own. The houses were quiet and all the shutters down, the windows and doors and dormant chimneys filing past in slow procession.

A warden nodded to him on the corner. The hat and the bucket. He gave them a little smile and let his tired eyes and his tired feet draw him drifting onward, treading softly all the way to his simple gate and simple path and simple, peeling door.

The key fiddled and stuck and eventually made up its mind. He stood under the single cone of light inside his narrow hall and slowly took off the different parts of the day. He left his boots by the door and his coat on its hook and he left his keys on the table by the wall. All squared away.

One last check of the lock and then he switched off the light and continued into the kitchen. There was the big refrigerator he had bought six years ago and it loomed out of the surrounding cabinets as if to say hello. He pulled it open and looked at the small tub of food that he had been allocated yesterday. It was lonely in the cavernous space. That was dinner then, eaten at the table, the only sound the slow chewing of his mouth.

The bed was cold. The clock ticked. His eyes did not want to shut. He rubbed at them and shifted and at some point it became morning, or close enough to morning. The light wiggled through the edges of his window frame and goaded him up and out and into the tepid water of the bath. Slosh and a thin scrape of soap. He scrubbed at his stained and cracking hands.

The walk to work and punching his card at the booth. The sound and heat wrapped around him and took him in. He stood on his section of the line and became a part of the machine. Here was metal and here was skin, like a robot man in the stories he used to read.

The stories were gone and it was important work and he should be proud to do it. He was proud to do it. Or it was better than the other thing. And a brave lad too. Anyone could see that.

They had a drill at lunch time and he stomped and hopped along and crouched down with the rest of them. The wounded and the women who had not yet been called up. For him, it was his leg, of course. Or the part of his leg that wasn't. Red fire and shattering noise and a ticket home.

Work finished and it seemed that not everything had been a drill and the road he usually took was closed off for now. He kept his eyes away and went over to the next street. The same brick and pavement and the same heavy silence. A child was out in one of the gardens and he waved at them and they went back inside.

He moved on. The sky was hung over with clouds

again. The houses filed past and in each one was a child that was not allowed to play. Then there was something different. A small, round window halfway up one wall. He stopped when he saw it, struck still by the strange beauty of the circular brick and the delicate wood that separated the small panes of glass.

It was the sort of beauty that wasn't seen or allowed anymore. The simple sight of it filled him with a strange and swelling feeling that drew him back to when he was a child himself. The sound of water and the bright sun and the rough feel of the wooden decking beneath his feet.

It had been a summer trip. A barge taken along the rivers and canals of the sunny, southern countryside. He remembered the sound of his father's voice as he taught him and his brother how to go about the boat and all the names of things. His own finger pointing at the window – so similar to this one – and asking what it was.

A porthole. He remembered holding the tiller and how it shook beneath his hand. The chugging motor and the green of the river banks and the farmer that had waved to them from his field. A smile spread out across his face and a tear ran down from one eye. His brother had gone across first and no ticket home. A small mound in a field of his own. His father drove dead-wagons and maybe still did. There was hardly any news anymore.

They had seen each other once, out there; he who had been a son and the man who had been his father. It had been a freak crossing of paths, as if someone was twisting the knife. Their eyes had met for a moment, dark-ringed eyes like devils, and they had not said a single word.

Home before curfew. He took off his boots and made his food and went upstairs to take off his leg. He rubbed at the round stump below the knee and those darker thoughts that usually came along were kept down by other memories of earlier days. There were happy things, he remembered. There had been happy things.

At night it was not as easy. The terror came on and took him. Hollow buildings and the walls leaning and the circle of brick a gaping mouth that –

He woke in a sweat. Shivering. He snatched upright, peeling back the window screen and looking in the direction of the street. No orange glow of fires or any dark plume of smoke. A deep breath and falling back towards bed. Without sleep of course, just lying there and waiting for the day.

The day came and he went to work. His hands moved. His mind stuck on the window. It must survive. It had to. It must.

Another raid came through and the sirens rang and for a moment he thought to run the other way, as though he might wrap his arms around the whole street and the whole world and hold it all in. But the factory warden shouted at him and dragged him along to the shelter and as the ceiling rattled and the dust came down, he tried to hide in the memories of the boat and the summer sound of laughter across the water.

Eventually it was over. They came out blinking into the nighttime and saw that it had been a bad one. Some of the factory was gone and the trees were burning in the park. They stood like a group of explorers on the edge of a strange planet, frail and unprepared, as sirens rang out on the other side of the city and the stabbing fire of searchlights and tracers destroyed the sky only a few miles away.

He walked into it as though in a dream. Slow and stumbling. The smoke caught at his throat and drew tears from his eyes. A fire-car steamed past to some important place somewhere, leaving the rest of it to burn. Maybe the war was lost and this was the last time. People running and the frantic shouting in the dark. He fell over something softer and could not bring himself to look. Everything here was gone. It was hard to believe how broken things could be. Even after all this time it was hard to believe. He dragged onwards, towards the street and the house and the window. The gaping vision and fire and a smouldering hole and his father gone and his brother gone and all of it gone for no reason that anyone could explain at all.

Yet somehow it was still there. Nestled between ruins, the house stood defiant or blessed or pure, stupid lucky. He stopped at the window and stared at it. Trying to feel something. Feeling nothing at all.

Then there were two eyes looking back at him and a little tuft of hair. Eyes like his eyes. Peering out. They watched each other and maybe it was a part of him behind that little window. A young boy who didn't know. He offered a smile to them, a thin smile just barely painted on, and wondered if it would be enough.

SKYE WILSON

Epithalamion i
19/03/22

If love is to be seen and really see,
to know and to be known, true love
is shown when Jade and Eli play charades.
They read each other's minds—
Love Actually, Les Misérables, Mulan—

until it gets too late, at 8pm
and they walk home, holding hands.
Jade & Eli's home is filled with elephants,
with home-cooked food & brewing tea,
with lavender and—always—love.
They carry it from Aberdeen
to Coral Beach; from strolls in Ceres

to earthquakes in Greece; from their home
to this hallowed room,
which knows they are eternal.
There is no end to their joy.

Today is love: each sound, each smile,
each dress and kilt and lipstick
in a handbag—all echoing
through the future you feel
in this moment; this moment
they will feel throughout their lives.

SKYE WILSON

Elegy i
23/03/22

My gran and grandpa meet at a dance in Ceres.
They spin and sparkle; waltz and twirl—she looks
into his eyes and sees their life: dancing
at their grandchildren's wedding, their brood
of twenty-seven, poetry and holidays
and too-short years of perfect happiness.
He drops her home, ablaze with possibility.

The spark she saw in him, that fire, only grew
throughout his life. It was always ready
to be shared: he passed on his passion
to my dad and brothers, shared his knowledge
with so many, gave his love to us all.
Today, we laugh and cry and recollect:
a lifetime full of stories; a fire burning on.

SKYE WILSON

Epithalamion ii
21/10/22

As the leaves blush and the harvest comes
we gather in this gorgeous place, a castle
for a fairytale. Today, the past and future
meet. Today, Josh and Shauna's vows
make themselves, and us, and the whole world
new, make it eternal. Today, we celebrate
the history of Josh and Shauna:

Halloweens and horseshoes; Hugo
and the Highland Show. We celebrate
their joy, and hope, and fearless love.
This love started with a heartbar shoe
with extra heel support—and then
a pause, a secret spark. This love
has led to a life together, of barbecues
and board games and adventures—

the biggest one of all is Harriet:
beautiful and clever like her mam;
mischievous and funny like her dad.
Their love has brought them here today,
lockdown-late, but what is one year
in all existence? Today is both history
and future, seeds sown and harvest grown
and gathered, enough here for a lifetime.

M.H. MONICA

Hey Eve

The crescent and stars provide little light to see the loose stones and sand under my feet, and I'm forced to proceed with caution. As the breeze gathers speed, I hope I don't catch a cold. I stash away my diving equipment and periscope in the anchored boat's locker. There is no sign of anyone along the shore – perfect. Clad the skimpiest bikini I packed, I head back to the hotel. Goosebumps cover every inch of my body despite the two thick beach towels I have wrapped around my shoulders and waist. My feet and hands are so cold that they have gone numb. I can't tell if it's the result of the wind or my midnight scuba-diving adventures.

My wet hair begins to curl up, water dripping down my back and onto the towel. It's hard to believe that just ten hours ago, it had been sweat dripping down my body. The unbearable heat forced me to stay indoors for most of the afternoon. The evening had proven to be even less fruitful. Walking down to the village market and doing the typical touristy shopping had led to nothing. Just old, wrinkly women glaring at me and saying, "No know English." Tending to travellers like me was clearly not a priority for the locals. Listening to them call me *oniranu* and *ode* behind my back was an additional treat. Who doesn't want to be told how dull and foolish they are.

Not that they realised I knew what they were saying...

But now, as I try to hurry back to the warmth of my room, elation makes my heart thump louder. Tonight was incredible. I can finally leave this wretched island and go back home. If another mosquito bites me, I swear to God!

The hotel looms ahead on the little windswept hill, the eerie glow spilling from its lobby windows the sole source of light. I can't believe the thatched roof hasn't blown away. Matter of fact, the yellowing walls shouldn't be standing either. But whatever stone the islanders used was clearly sturdy enough to last over 75 years.

Could Marco have returned to the front desk already? Better to go in the back; I can't afford to be seen. Not tonight. Peering through the windows, I make my way. Some of the curtains are drawn, and the darkness inside the others doesn't allow me to make out a single thing. With a sigh, I keep going, trying not to slip out of my flip-flops and twist my ankles as I inch forward. Nothing like the sound of squelching slippers in the dead of night to slow down progress. I miss my sneakers...

The key under the planter is missing. I feel my stomach lurch. What do I do now? Out of sheer hope, I push the back door and it creaks open. Huh! It's just one piece of luck after another tonight.

Slipping in, I am slowly closing the door behind me when something squeaks past my foot. In an effort not to scream, I shirk away and give an airy gasp as the rat disappears down the corridor. A loud click turns on the hallway light. I nearly jump out of my skin but have the sense to loosen the towel around my waist so that, as I turn, it falls to the ground, revealing my outfit.

Marco stands by the switch, looking as unimpressed

as ever, but I can see his eyes dart over my body before settling on my sheepish smile.

As I start on my rehearsed excuse, Marco yells, "What you doing here, Miss?"

I flinch. The vein on his forehead is throbbing. "I just went for a midnight swim..." I try to bat my eyes at him, but he just grunts. Time to change strategies. I swoop down and pick up my fallen towel, making sure he gets a nice view.

"Swim? This time in night? You crazy, Miss?!"

"Don't people swim at night here? You know, go skinny dipping?" I wrap the fallen towel around my shoulders in such a way as to push my breasts together. He gulps a little. Bingo.

"No swimming in night. No sneaking in night. Sneaking only for thieves and bad people," Marco says with finality. "Now go and wear warm clothes or you fall sick."

"Aww, you care about me." I give him a coy pat on the shoulder as I pass him. He nearly jumps out of my way.

"Breakfast at 7 sharp, Miss. No be late or no breakfast."

"Are you going to make something delicious for me?"

Marco looks serious for a second as he considers this. "I make special dinner. If you feel adventurous, I make very special dinner for just you tomorrow."

"Oh, Marco, that would be wonderful! Dinner just you and me then?" I grab his arm with a smile.

He pulls away in absolute horror. "Y-Yes, yes. Tomorrow at 8, dinner."

"Now, don't watch me as I walk away, Marco. Or do." I shrug and strut down the hall.

Climbing up the stairs, I can hear him muttering about crazy flirting foreigners in Yoruba. I grin at my own cheek.

The upstairs corridors are lit by a single dull bulb that shines over my head at the landing. Making my way as softly as possible, I pick up my room key from below my neighbour's doormat. My room welcomes me with a gust of warm air, and I take several deep breaths as I try to calm the adrenaline rush. What was Marco talking about, making a special dinner for me? There was definitely something off about that. Was he planning on catching some fugu? He definitely doesn't seem trained in the art of cooking it. Do they even have fugu in this region? The only fugu I remember reading about here are some traditional menswear. Hmm, maybe I'm just overthinking it...

Walking across the room, I shed the beach towels and brush sand off the random places it tends to get into – always behind the knees and between the buttcheeks for some reason. All the things on my table remain as I left them – my make-up, my travel journal, my wallet – except for my laptop. It isn't placed at the right angle. I freeze. This is no time to panic, yet the adrenaline comes rushing back, leaving me feeling a bit dizzy.

I pick up my compact powder from the table and pretend to look at my face as I press the button on the side. A small red light blinks twice at the hinge of the compact and stops.

Cameras. Shit.

•

there are NO MISTAKES, just BIG adventures!

Hey Eve,

I am having So much fun here. When will you join me At The hotel? i have been here a week now and Can't wait to show you this Huge Island. the people here are the Nicest! i have Got to show you My favourite... Everything!

Dare i say though, Rats can be a problem. Unless you're bringing a Giant cat, get your vaccines just to be Safe. And bring sunscreen! the Rays will End us! Instead of Nightwear, get more swimwear. the waters here are the Best! Aquamarine reefs, and golden Sands - what an Escape from the Mundane! Every Night, i have been hitting the Tide. swimming at night is such a peaceful activity, away from the sunlight.

i did get in trouble with the innKeeper for it though. he saw me Enter through the back door and Yelled at me. said there's no sneaking around on the Island at Night. what a Jerk! As if i was up to some Mischief. Just because he runs the place, doesn't mean he has an Absolute say in what i do. Right? he isn't bad-looking actually, and can be sweet, but what a temper. you'll see for yourself when you get here.

Breakfast, lunch, and dinner include freshly caught seafood from the Reef. it's Incredible! Nothing compares, not the Greatest five Star hotels. the Quality! i've gotten to eat something exotic and Unbelievable every day. the innkeeper has said he'll get me something very unique tomorrow if i feel extra Adventurous. a dinner for just him and me! can't wait to see what he has in store for me!

xoxo
Diane

TESS SIMPSON

The Witch Bone

We were told that the dead could not touch us, and that was the only thing that held our fear at bay. At night we huddled together, the three of us in one small bed, and tried not to listen to the darkness as it whispered our names.

It was my father who showed me the way to see them. You took one of their bones and drilled a hole right through. When you held the bone up and put your eye to the hole, the dead were visible again. Pale, grasping creatures in some place beyond the physical world. While you held their bones, you could see them as they can always see us.

My mother's finger bone hung above our door, but when my father took it down and handed it to me, I couldn't bring myself to look through the hole. At first.

My father never spoke of her. My siblings barely remembered her. I was the eldest and even my memories were clouded. They were the memories of a child who didn't realise that something so fundamental as a mother could be lost. My memories of my mother were the flotsam of a shipwreck, almost all drifted beyond my reach to the open sea.

The house we lived in was small, with a roof that leaked when it rained and gaps that whistled with the winter winds. When I made the mistake of asking about my mother, my father would look at me with a flat, blank expression and the walls seemed to shrink still further around me. I learned not to ask questions; and indeed, there was little time to. There were meals to cook and fires to build and children to tend to. The twins always cried, one setting off the other. I tried to comfort them as our mother would, but it was their birth that had killed her. In my worst moments, I longed to trade them back for her.

The twins never cried at night, when the ghosts came calling. They would laugh and wave their fat little hands to the whispering darkness. Their lack of fear only made me more afraid, as the house creaked around me, and my father paced next door, and the cruel, cold wind whispered underneath the thin blankets. The women of the village already disliked the twins, and whispers of ghost-talking would only make matters worse.

There were stories about my mother's death. The only people who knew what happened the night the twins were born were my father and the old midwife who attended all the births in the village. We other children were banished from the house as soon as she arrived, laden with strong-smelling herbs, barely sparing us a glance.

'Get the wee 'uns out of here,' she muttered, pushing past us, huddled at the foot of the stairs, drawn deeper into the house by my mother's screams. She had been screaming for so long before the midwife came. I took my younger brother and sister each by the hand and led them out to the woods. We scrounged for early blackberries and late summer flowers to give to our mother when we got home. As the light began to fail and there was no call for us from the doorway of our house, we settled on a grassy bank that butted against the spread roots of a big beach tree. The ground was littered with dusty nuts and empty shells, and as my siblings played at fairy tea, I watched the doorway of our house and waited.

The call never came. Eventually, chilled by the early autumn cold, I left my brother and sister drowsing beneath the tree and crept back to the house. As I stepped over the threshold, I heard the cries of the twins for the first time. There was something wrong in the air. No other noise – no talking, no laughter, no murmured conversation. I snuck to the door of my parents' room and peered inside.

I saw the broad back of my father. I saw the midwife, leaning over a wicker basket. I saw the bed, and the lumpy shape that was covered by the sheets. I saw the red staining them and I smelled the iron in the air.

This is the point when my memory folds in on itself, the moment the ship crashes into the rocks. I can remember none of the days that followed with any sort of clarity. The next thing I remember is the day after my mother's funeral, when my father came into the house with a priest and my mother's finger bone. He and the priest vanished into the bedroom where the twins had been born and my mother had died. The smell of incense started to fill the house, and the priest's wailing chants set the babies off, screaming in sympathy. After the priest left, my father hung the finger bone over our front door, and it stayed there from that moment on.

Until the night my father took it down and told me to put my eye to the hole just above the knuckle.

The voice curled across my mind like the smoke of a blown-out candle.

Look at me.

My father was next to me, his hands a vice on my shoulders. I wanted to turn away, but he would not let me go. I saw her, nothing more than a pale concentration of air. She was standing just outside the door, reaching for me, her arms unnaturally long. I recoiled and my father let me, his hands loosening their grip as I lurched away and dropped the bone to the floor.

I was shaking, but all my father did was pick the bone up and place it back above the door. When he turned away, there was grim satisfaction on his face.

After that night, I could never think of my mother without hearing that voiceless plea and seeing those long arms reaching towards me. Sometimes I would wake and see the twins, cooing at the darkness, and I would shudder and repress the urge to sweep them out of the cot and into the shadows.

It was the women at the marketplace who saved me. The same ones who glared suspiciously at the twins. They had seen the attention my father was paying to the young daughter of the baker, a girl only a few years my senior.

'Thinks she's lucky now, but just wait. Marta had a time with him, and she'll be getting it as well if he and her father have their way. Weren't just the babies who killed her, if old Jessamin was to be believed.'

'Refused to go back to that house she did, even with the two bairns fresh from the oven and no ma to tend them. Said some funny business went on that night. Said Marta'd still be here if she'd been able to keep him out of the delivery room.'

I was bursting to hear more, but the twins started to cry and I hurried away before the women could turn their gazes on me.

I waited until my father stopped pacing, and I could hear the rumble of his snores through the wall. I got up and crept to the front door. This time when I looked through the hole in the bone I was ready, and though the pale thing in front of me still reached out with long thin arms, I had tended my courage enough to overcome the fear.

Look at me.

And this time I did. I did not run or try to turn my face away. I stepped forward, still holding the bone up to my eye, out of the house and into the trees we had sheltered beneath all those months ago. She was less unnatural in the moonlight, out of the human world of stone and straw.

'What happened to you?' I asked, and in answer, she sighed.

Look at me.

That night I walked back in the house and woke my younger brother and sister. We took the twins out of their wicker basket and they smiled and waved at the shadows which crowded around us. We took blankets and clothes and food, and then we left, heading from our house into the welcoming darkness of the forest. I was the last to leave. My father's snores echoed from the room where he slept, the room my mother had died in. I turned my face to the sky and dropped the torch I was carrying. The rush matting caught light so quickly; the fire ran in a straight line towards the bedroom. As I left I laid the finger down on the threshold, so the fire could do its work. I knew, you see, that what it burns it can also set free. Then I turned my back on the man who killed my mother and walked away as his house burned to the ground.

KATHARINA KÖRBER

Self-Portrait as Translation

My dreams don't speak
My mother's language, my voice
Inflects between dictionaries
Chanting everything and nothing
      alles und nichts.
Like saint's bones, I carry myself across
The othered line of questioning
How does one translate oneself?

I exchange uvulars for alveolars
Air out the vowels, rescue the *R*
From the depths of my throat.
I explain what the *Umlaut* means in airports
To avoid trouble and mould one expression
Out of a whole sentence and back, juggle
The simile of self with at least two arms missing
And smile at everyone who nods at me
In either understanding or disbelief –
Who knows
What language they speak
To themselves when no one is listening.

I am the snake with the forked tongue
Not to be imported
Under the Endangered Species Act.
I am the space between the chairs
        where we sit
The non-belongers,
The extra-large baggage claimers
Shivering upwards, splitting biology:
Half human, fully vertebrate
Being both and neither,
    beides und doch keines
All at once.

KATHARINA KÖRBER

Grandmother's Garden

I never wanted this, you
dripping rain all over the front room, sleep-deprived
and shivering for a heat that will not be rekindled
after climbing a tree you are now too big for
to bring the apples home and butcher them,
peel them too wide and wasteful to the point it hurts.

> I didn't have the heart to tell you, Granny
> that the storm picked up your favourite branch
> and ran with it, all roars and splintered juice.
> The wet grass soaked my shoes
> the next morning as I saw and wept
> for all we lost, you and me.

When I shut the years out, I can still see you
sitting up there with your harvest mirrored
in your pupil skies, all ripeness and smiles.
You were not ready for the world
to let you down, my little girl
I wanted to keep you in this garden forever.

KATHARINA KÖRBER

Rheumatoid Android

I am the joint between a tale and an audience
Made up of seventy percent water.
A projection surface is a mirror not a person.

                I am my mother's child, her tears
                Lick my pleura on the dark days.
    Methotrexate, Sulfasalazine, I chant medical poetry.

Guilt knows no middle ground.
I am not broken, but – saviours
Stay in stories close to your heart.

                I am my own responsibility. Some
                days all the colours bleed into
                Each other and turn to grey sheets.

I am a dysfunctional puzzle,
Ten thousand pieces all the same shade
Of impossibility and stubbornness, copiously inherited.

                Emotion starts with motion after all.
          If there is a line between health and sickness
                You can call me a tightrope walker.

MEGAN WILLIS

Vague Prophecy

Taking the ends of the fortune cookie, I snap it like a wishbone.

The view of the Royal Mile from the restaurant is the same as from my flat above, although at this level, I can clearly see the faces behind the wheels of the cars travelling infrequently down the cobbles. Dinner is never normally this late, but I've been told not to eat in the morning. The one waiter that's left kills the background music so the only sound is the drumming of rain. Minutes before, I had avoided his gaze but he brought the bill anyway, unsmiling.

I sigh and unroll the paper with a silent prayer, unaddressed. My heart falters.

The fortune is blank, like an unsold gravestone.

Upstairs, I come in quietly and leave the door ajar, trying to catch my breath without wheezing before straightening up. My back aches. The metal lock snaps into place.

A silhouette appears in the darkness of my bedroom doorway and my mind floods with accusations of ghosts, but then the light flicks on and it's only my sister. Well, half-sister. She's holding a pile of my clothes, all neatly folded. I have to stop myself from snapping at her for touching them, remind myself she's doing me a favour by being here.

'Jean,' she says, her voice that honeyed, sticky posh type of English. 'You're back rather late.' Catherine is the only person who calls me by my given name. She thinks nicknames are common.

'Kitty,' I reply. Her lip twitches.

'I've been to the supermarket,' she says. Brisk. Straight to business. 'I bought easy things as you suggested. Tins of soup and microwave meals, though I can't say they look appetising.' She smiles tightly. 'I also noticed that you hadn't packed, so I made a start.'

In my cramped bedroom, Catherine walks across the old wooden floorboards and places the clothes into the battered suitcase on my bed. The sight of the thing makes my chest tighten. As I sink down beside the case, I fidget with my wedding ring. Through the months of loneliness and longing, I have kept it on. My fingers tremble. Catherine doesn't seem to notice.

Though we share blood, there is nothing in our appearances to suggest it. We both look like our mothers. Even our family name betrays nothing – my feminist ma had insisted I take hers. She'd been young and idealistic when I was born. Our dad had been the same, for a time, before he fucked off back to London. All three parents have been in the ground for years, so I guess it's really no matter who we look like, but it's once in a blue moon we see each other and these things always occur to me like new. How long's it been? I count back. Ten months since my wife's funeral.

'Would you like to take a book?' Catherine asks, nodding at the shelves cluttered with paperbacks. She's in the corner of the room now, down to folding the last of the clothes that have been piled there for weeks. God knows what's clean and what's worn. I had thought to shift them before Catherine arrived, but couldn't find the strength.

I stare at the rows of cracked spines. In pride of place on one shelf is a gold-framed photograph of Shona and me on Portobello Beach, our arms around one another, our smiling lips about to touch. In the matte-finished image, it's dreich out. My hair is whipping wildly around my face. Shona's is gone completely.

The empty fortune is a lead weight on my mind, pinning me to the spot.

'I can't go.'

Catherine's hands freeze mid-fold. 'Excuse me?'

Her tone is sharp. I cross my arms to shield from it, jut my chin out. I bite my lip to stop it trembling. 'I said, I'm not going.'

Catherine drops the fabric and crosses her arms too. We face each other, the same stubborn image but distorted, like a funhouse mirror.

'You cannot be serious.'

'Why not?'

'It is not up for negotiation,' she replies, exasperated.

'Aye,' I agree coolly, 'it isn't.'

We stay locked in position. Catherine starts tapping her foot, so I do the same.

But I won't meet her eye. Something shifts. She uncrosses her arms, as if she's read my thoughts.

'Jean, you look terribly pale. Has something happened?'

The sudden softness catches me off guard.

'You wouldn't understand.'

'I see.' Catherine stands there, slim arms hanging by her sides. I wait for her to move, but she doesn't. I can tell by the slight crease between her thin brows that she isn't sure what to do with herself, and there is something about this gesture that convinces me.

So I tell her the truth about the blank paper, about how it feels like an omen. A foreshadowing. Someone as stubbornly logical as Catherine would never respect superstition, so when I'm done I prepare myself to be picked apart. I expect that sharp tone of hers to voice the thoughts I'm trying to ignore. That I'm off my head. That I need to get a grip.

'Are you certain it was a *bad* omen?' she says instead. She lowers herself elegantly onto the bed beside me. The breath I've been holding in rushes out.

'What'd you mean?'

'Well,' Catherine begins slowly, 'an omen can be good or bad. It all depends on perspective.' The uncertainty in her expression clears suddenly. She snaps her fingers. 'Like Halley's Comet.'

'Eh?'

'The comet was an ill omen for King Harold II, who died at the Battle of Hastings and lost the English throne, but a good one for William the Conqueror, who claimed it.'

'England? Sure the luck wasn't the other way round?'

'Point is,' Catherine continues, 'the comet was a sign of change; an ending, or a new beginning, depending on how you interpret it.'

I let the words sink in.

'You always ken the weirdest things.'

She shrugs. There's an awkward pause and I'm not sure how to fill the silence. Apparently, neither is she.

Then a thought occurs. 'Seems it's only after the things happened that you can tell what the omen meant for who.' My voice is steady, but only just. 'How'd I ken if mine is good or bad, before…?'

For once, Catherine doesn't know the answer.

Not a foreshadowing, then. A vague prophecy.

Catherine stands and continues moving around the room, putting slippers and socks into the suitcase, though I haven't said I've changed my mind back, that I'll go.

'How about that book?' she asks eventually.

I shake my head and swallow, the sound loud in my ears. 'I'll take the photo, though.'

She passes the gold frame into my outstretched hand. I want to squeeze my eyes shut and press my forehead to the glass, pretending, as I have on lonelier nights, that it is a portal to the past. But I don't, not with Catherine here.

I simply say: 'I always told her she'd break my heart.'

Morning comes. An ungodly hour.

On the ghost-town street, the suitcase's wheels on the cobbles break the silence. As we pass St Giles' Cathedral, I spit instinctively on the heart-shaped mosaic at the feet of Walter Montagu Douglas Scott's statue. The Heart of Midlothian: a stone heart that has beat strong in the Mile's chest for centuries. I envy its strength.

'It's good luck,' I explain when I catch Catherine's quick look of distaste. 'Like rubbing Bobby's nose.'

She joins me at the heart's edge, the click of her heels a drumroll at fractional speed. Without looking at me, she holds her dark hair behind her ears and spits delicately on target.

The entrance to the Infirmary is all white panels and grey sky reflected in glass.

Inside, I can almost taste the hospital smell,

antiseptic half-masked under something bitter and artificial. A flimsy identity bracelet that reminds me of the festival wristbands of my youth scratches at my skin as a consultant who is so very young, with thin-framed glasses and kind eyes, helps me prepare for the procedure. Body piercings, make-up and nail polish are removed. I have never felt more naked. I shower, put on a polyester hospital gown.

Catherine is allowed as far as the ward, where she waits with me in silence. But I must go to the operating theatre alone.

I struggle to stay present as the surgeon goes over the details of my surgery.

'As you are undergoing a triple bypass, the surgery will last around five or six hours. Anaesthetic will be administered. We will begin by harvesting veins from various extremities for the bypass grafts.' My mind flits back to the pre-admission assessment, days before, where the surgeon spoke in that same swift and graphic manner.

They asked me questions about my medical history, my home circumstances. Someone would have to stay with me during my recovery. Panic choked me.

'Blood vessels will be taken from your saphenous vein, your internal mammary artery, or your radial artery, which are in your leg, chest and arm respectively.'

Endless tests: blood count, chest x-ray, an electrocardiogram. They put small electrodes on my arms, legs and chest to record the electrical signals my heart was producing.

'Once all the graft vessels have been removed, we will make a cut down the middle of your chest so that we can divide your breastbone and access your heart.'

The consultant said we needed to discuss possible complications of the surgery. Infection. Stroke. Heart attack. He had a duty to consult me in relation to precautionary medical provisions. The form he handed me had different sections. Recording a statement of beliefs. Appointing a health care proxy, for if I could no longer make a decision for myself.

'We will stop your heart; we cannot work on a moving target. A heart-lung bypass machine will supply oxygen to your blood and pump it through your body. Once the grafts are complete, we will restart your heart using controlled electric shocks.'

One circumstance where this could be needed, listed in bold, was: persistent unconsciousness, with no likelihood of regaining.

'Voluntary written consent is required to proceed.'

The blank space on the page, waiting for my signature, gives me déjà vu. I shove the feeling away and sign. After this, it's all pretty straightforward. A mask over my mouth and nose that pumps pure oxygen. Drugs into a vein in the back of my hand. I can't feel this but know it's happening, and I flex my fingers out instinctively as if reaching for a comforting touch, though none comes. At Shona's bedside, in those last days at the hospice, her hands had looked almost blue. There had been restlessness, confusion, hallucinations and much worse for her. At least this would not be that. But what is the alternative? More days at the empty flat, watching strangers on the Mile from my window, only now with a heart that works? Maybe I'll ask Catherine to visit more.

One way or the other, there will be a change. That is the only thing of which I am certain. The faces around me blur. I cling to consciousness like fingertips curled stiff round a cliff's edge.

Then I breathe out softly. I let go.

My eyes fall shut under the paper-white light.

ABIGAIL O'NEILL

Cinnamon Rolls

Step one: preheat the oven to 180 degrees Celsius.

It just turned up on my doorstep this morning.
 What, like it was just there?
 Yeah. Just … right there.
 And you didn't throw it away?
 Dude. Look at it.
 In Dan's hand, there was the perfect scroll of a cinnamon roll. It was golden, slightly browned, glistening through the icing and tinged lilac from the cling film it had been wrapped in.
 I don't trust it, Hari said, tapping his fingers on Dan's desk. Do you trust it?
 I'm not sure. It's definitely a bit strange, but still, it looks really good? Like, feel that …
 Dan pushed the side of it carefully, leaving a slight indentation before it bounced back again.
 As instructed, Hari copied him.
 Damn. That's like the perfect amount of squidginess.
 Exactly.
 But still, Dan. Come on. You shouldn't eat something that's just been left on your doorstep.
 Not in my current flat. I mean, I do live in Bethnal Green.
 Hari laughed and grabbed the roll. Sure you don't

want to give it to Bill in finance? You know him, he'll eat anything, he said.

Dan laughed, but shook his head. The roll made a slight thud as it dropped into the empty bin.

I wonder what the cleaners will make of that one this evening, Hari said.

Step two: combine the dry ingredients. Add the wet ingredients and mix. Knead until the dough is smooth and doesn't stick to the surface. Leave to prove.

The next morning, Dan made a beeline for Hari's desk as soon as he got into the office. Hari must have been invested in his spreadsheet, as he jumped, startled, when Dan dropped the cinnamon roll into his overflowing in-tray.

Are you joking, Hari said, clutching at his heart and feigning an attack.

Nope! Dan picked the cinnamon roll back up and held it carefully between his palms.

Another one?

Yes. He rolled a lifting corner of cling film between his forefinger and thumb.

Let me have a closer look at this thing, Hari said.

No, Dan flinched, pulling it out of Hari's reach.

Bloody hell mate, it's just a cinnamon roll –

Yeah. But knowing you, you'll throw it out again before I've had a chance to stop you.

Jesus, Dan. Why don't you just go to Pret and get one you know isn't going to poison you?

But this one looks so perfect.

Dan, no offence, but it's probably some rubbish that a fox has dropped. Yes, two days in a row is a bit weird, but if a fox has decided it doesn't want it twice, then you definitely shouldn't eat it.

Squinting slightly, Dan examined the cling film that encased the bun. I see no teeth marks, he said.

Hari's eyes widened. You're weirder than I thought you were, he said, turning his attention back to his spreadsheet.

Tapping his foot on the floor, Dan flipped the roll over in his hands a few times before heading back to his own desk and placing it carefully in the top drawer.

Step three: combine the butter, cinnamon and sugar to form a paste.

Dan hesitated before stepping outside – the previous two days he'd almost crushed the parcels on his way out. There it was. He smiled, pleased at not making the same mistake. But today, there was a small, lilac sticky-note on it that read 'eat me' with a small smiley face and a heart. He traced the lettering, it was small, neat, and almost like a font, but with gentle swoops which proved it to be handwritten. Lifting the paper to his face, he found himself sniffing in search for some other clue. A trace of perfume? There was nothing, but he could almost hear a woman whispering to him, filling his chest with warmth as the morning sunlight glistened onto his doorway.

Step four: roll out the dough to form a rectangle. Spread over the paste and twist it into a scroll. Slice into twelve portions. Leave to prove.

Dan's stomach growled as he sat at his desk. Maybe just a taste, he thought. That wouldn't do any harm. Three days in a row couldn't be a coincidence. He peeled back a corner of the cling film and instantly the room smelled like a bakery. Carefully, he took a bite, chewing slowly as if he might start frothing at the mouth. When nothing happened, he took another. That's when it hit him.

The sumptuously soft sweetened dough, with the occasional crunch of sugar crystals from the filling, was perfectly balanced by the slightly sour cream cheese frosting that had oozed into the creases of the coil. Each bite made the room around him become foggier, as he unravelled the roll and explored the layers of flavours that his beautiful, mysterious baker had introduced him to.

Did you just scoff that whole thing? Hari asked, eyebrow raised.

Dan's heart stuttered. He looked up at Hari with his finger in his mouth, licking some of the icing from underneath his fingernail. On his desk, all that was left were finger smears on the cling film.

Uh, I guess I did.

Well, while we wait and see if you do keel over, we need to talk about tomorrow's meeting. For the presentation –

Hari continued to talk at him, and Dan nodded in all the right places, but inwardly he was fishing out whatever remnants he could find lodged in his molars. He checked the time; only twenty hours until another cinnamon roll would be waiting on his doorstep for him. Or, he could check the bins to see if the previous ones were still in there ... No, he thought, catching himself. He could be patient. He could wait until the morning. He might even be able to sneak a look at who had been leaving them for him. Twenty ... Nineteen more hours.

Step five: bake the buns for thirty-five minutes. Leave to cool in the tray. Combine the cream cheese frosting ingredients until smooth. Spread evenly over the cinnamon rolls.

Cinnamon Rolls / 111

5:30am. There were two hours left on his mental timer, and he sat, poised, looking through the gap between the window and his curtains. He'd checked his doormat half an hour ago, and there was nothing there, so she couldn't have stopped by yet.

As he waited, his mind was occupied with the thoughts of the cinnamon roll that awaited him. He couldn't wait to feel the heaviness of it in his hands. Today, he would be more mindful. More careful. He'd rushed through eating it yesterday, barely noticing the intricacies of the experience. He wouldn't be so careless again.

There was a fray on his shorts; he mindlessly twisted the fabric between his finger and thumb as he sat on the floor behind his sofa, keeping his eyes on the doorway. It was getting lighter outside, the sun just creeping over the surrounding blocks of flats.

Almost level with his excitement for his breakfast was his anticipation to see who his baker was. He'd tried to picture her, but all he could envision was a woman with perfectly manicured fingernails – lilac, just like the post-it note – scooping the ingredients into the bowl, winding the dough into a ball, rolling it carefully out with a ceramic rolling pin and twisting each bun into a small piece of perfection. Small clouds of flour would puff into the air, settling down into her apron which she'd tied loosely around her waist. He could almost feel his hands around her, standing behind and cradling her while she baked. Her neck would smell like vanilla, from the extract, but also just because. When his lips brushed against her, she would turn in his arms, focussing on him now, and her lips would taste like sugar too –

The metal stairs outside clattered as someone made their way down. He held his breath, but it was a man who walked by, not noticing Dan, hunched over in the window. The sunlight scattered across the floor, skittering rays dancing on the boards each time someone walked by and disturbed the rays that shone through his front-door window panes.

From the bedroom, Dan heard his phone vibrating. As he moved to stand, a woman with glistening blonde hair stopped at the end of the walkway, rummaging through her bag. He heard the phone vibrate until it clattered onto the floor. She took a few steps closer towards his door. His breath caught in his throat. She looked around. Dan was frozen, his calves cramping slightly from this half-sitting, half-standing position. What was in her bag, he wondered? Today's cinnamon roll?

She pivoted and rushed back up the stairs; he had just enough time to go, grab his phone and be back in his spot before she returned.

Fifteen texts and seven missed calls from Hari. What did he want? Then the texts revealed themselves: he was half an hour late to their presentation and, seemingly, Hari was becoming increasingly concerned about him. The most recent read: Can you just let me know you're okay?! Looking at the time, he noticed it was 9:30. Had he really sat there for four hours?

Dan's feet went numb. Their meeting, which they'd been planning for weeks. The room spun; his job, or cinnamon rolls for the rest of his life? A grunt escaped as he stuffed himself into a suit, tried to smooth down his hair, and threw a mint into his mouth. He could always watch out for her tomorrow.

Through the dread, a bubble of excitement floated within his stomach at the thought of opening his door and finding a parcel of perfection. Truly, an impeccable breakfast before he begged Hari – and their boss – for another chance.

Somewhere between being in a rush and being careful, Dan opened the door. He didn't want to squash it. Except, there was nothing there.

The stairs creaked, and he could see her coat as she turned onto the street below.

Hey! He shouted, leaning over the railing opposite his door. You forgot –

But she didn't turn around. She didn't even hear.

He turned to see his reflection in the glass panel. Empty-handed.

YANG YUE

The Posthumous Letter

It is a suicide note that disappears as it is written. As the extra components like signal transmitters and chips are removed from my body piece by piece, the feeling of waves lapping at my ankles fades. So it is the virtual world again. It's artistic, isn't it? A book of last words, at the end of the world, left behind.

To hide a great secret, would you choose to control individuals, or would you choose to control the network of connections between them? The world has too many secrets.

I look over at the man who is operating on me. The illumination is similar to the feeling of the beach sun earlier. His serious, tight brow fascinates me a little, even though he is the Pain Maker. It is happening again. I smile bitterly.

When I first met this man, my eyes were swollen from crying over a woman. She was my best friend in the VR game, and when we were working together on quests, she kept asking me questions like "why has this painter lost his desire to live" and "is there really a planet where you can see the sunset forty-four times," and I always lost my breath staring into her icy blue irises, which represented the Rational Faction; even if they were virtual images, they were beautiful and reminded you of tall glaciers.

So different from my red irises, the Emotional Faction. I should be grateful. I should thank her for that because, before, I was asked very few questions in a world where everything was set in stone: food preferences, suitable mates, the possibility of diseases, rationalists or emotionalists ... genes will tell you, all written in the file when people do their tests after birth. For too long, no one asked, and I became the clam that didn't talk.

I often suspected she was there to spy on me, like a task assigned to me by the system; these tasks seemed random, but looking closer, you'd realise they were all about writing game experience reports for rationalists who couldn't tell if the blue eyes were happy or unhappy from their facial expressions. At the beginning of my memory, I did enjoy meeting different people in the game after work. At that time, I was working as a memory erasure auditor. Completing the mandatory game missions of the federal government seemed to open up a second life, and those games with a romantic air dissolved the bitterness of the real world.

But that day, she hugged me from behind. She breathed on my neck, and goosebumps instantly took over half of my body. I ignored the "sanity points" for the three-week-long mission that was due and asked to be forced out of the game. Before I could unplug the cable, I tumbled out of the recliner and began to vomit. Didn't my genes tell the monitors that I was in need of mental stimulation rather than physical stimulation? Especially after recognising that the purpose of this forced game was to take control of us, the overexposure made me feel sick and desperate.

My followbot, Happy Dog, came over with a red alert light on its chest and gave me a shot. I don't remember much after the injection, except that after I calmed down, I hugged Happy Dog and cried, yelling and crying, and it patted me on the back and gently wiped my tears, as it usually does.

When I woke up, a man was slapping me vigorously on the cheek to keep me awake. At first, the bright yellow light and clean white walls made me think I had been uploaded to work.

"Do me a favour." His eyes were icy blue, yet not so cold, so I froze and said what was on my mind, "You're on the rational side..."

He spoke very fast and picked up my words, "A director of the Rational Faction, Genetic Monitoring Division of the Science and Technology Bureau."

I laid back down on the floor. "Not interested." Oddly enough, several tears slid down my cheeks.

"Do you remember yet?" He was a little impatient and crossed his arms. "It's mutually beneficial. You won't say no."

I noticed a ruby ring on the second segment of his right pinky, and its light confronted my red eyes.

It was a strange feeling. Suddenly, there were a lot of people burrowing into my brain. I knew they weren't coming in through the strands of hair, but I couldn't help but hold my head and make sure it was okay, that it was still there – I had loved a lot of people, and the knowledge of that sent shivers through my body.

"Time is tight, so I won't wait for you to reminisce." His voice forced me to stay in this space. "You can develop strong empathy, even love, from watching someone else's painful memories while working."

"Jie..." The last girl who made me empathise to the point of tears and love to the point of heartbreak. Watching her memories was a sweet torture …

"It's a good thing you're too much of a coward to hurt someone by admiring their pain. That's why I passed your assessment report before you took the job." With that, he dragged me up off the floor and my legs went limp and weak. When I got a good look at the red-haired woman lying on the memory-clearing table, I flinched in shock. She looked like she was asleep. But I knew something was going to happen.

"I want my Happy Dog." I started to cry.

He put me in the chair by the console. "You trust the followbot too much."

"I want my Happy Dog." Each word shook off more tears.

He slumped down at the other end of the interface, folded his arms over his chest, closed his eyes and said, "You really haven't noticed. Don't you feel like you're missing half of your life?"

Missing? Is there a bigger lie to my life? I was reminded of those people ... the quivering wrinkles around their eyes ...

"Although I can't understand it, your ability to empathise makes you perfect for this job. Even if it has the side effect of making you fall in love with someone else as well as not being able to live a normal life, because those people won't remember you after they clear their painful memories."

Pain is the original sin, and I keep mending the web of memories in the hope of atoning for it. Those forgotten moments always drop my emotions below the warning line ...

"Your emotions are up and down so much that you stay under the alert long enough to try to kill yourself, but Happy Dog will show up just in time."

Happy Dog would show up in time to erase my memory.

He opened his eyes and stared at me. "That's probably why the two factions watch each other's backs. Perfect rule."

His eyes were so cold. But reality was colder.

"I can grant your wish."

My wish: liberation, which means to stop thinking, to stop feeling, which means to die.

"I need to know why." I began to operate the apparatus, as I had always done.

He took the redhead's hand and, surprisingly, rubbed it for a moment. The redhead was wearing a long white dress, with lace running from the fishtail hem to the neckline. He said, "According to the rules, to get promoted, you have to be an absolutely sane person. And I've done something I shouldn't have."

The apparatus was already running, and with that, the signal was tapped into my brain. Their memory storage area unfolded before my eyes. I asked in surprise, "Did you cheat on your wife?" His memories showed his wife with dark hair and a gentle face.

The corners of his mouth tugged upwards as if he had finally relaxed, and he said, "You'll see if you look a little longer."

The red-haired woman had his mother's face, with a beauty spot at the right corner of her mouth. A perfect replica – and even for someone belonging to the rational faction, it must be disconcerting to come face to face with his mother's clone like this. Her memories kept unfolding – they were not of a mother and her son. In this innocent lady's eyes, he was the perfect lover, with no other faults than being busy at work.

The Posthumous Letter / 119

He has been having an affair with a clone of his mother.

I began to tremble, like a pervert.

It looked like an old memory, and I was tempted to slow it down, but the components looked so worn out that I couldn't move them anymore.

His memories had now taken us all the way back into his childhood. I saw his grandparents arguing with his mother, a hammer coming down onto her forehead, again and again, until her beautiful forehead was sunken, until the mole on her mouth disappeared, until her and his world turned red. Had his mother's blood splashed into his eyes? His grandparents buried the broken body in the garden, escaping the law for many years. But he didn't know which corner of the yard. Every step he took on the grass felt on his mother's body, her broken body.

In those slow, long years, he recalled every detail over and over again. The look on his grandparents' faces, his mother's cries, the time on the wall clock.

Eleven forty at night.

His brow furrowed as I played this part of the memory, and he couldn't stop his arm from twitching. My hand, wiping the tears from my eyes, kept shaking too.

"This is why you became a rule-first rationalist over the centuries," I said softly.

Still holding her hand, he said, "Let's clear her memory first. I want to return her to a normal life."

I was puzzled. "Why go to all this trouble to maintain these pretences when you have the right to give a clone a normal identity?"

"People with many weaknesses are equally unable to understand people with only one." He finally let go of her hand and slipped the ruby ring over her pinky finger.

"Don't think of me as stupid ... I'm suited to memory

auditing because of my sensibility, but because of empathic pain, I want to escape; you've become suited to the work of rationalists because of the pain of your childhood, when you became rule-first. But again, pain becomes weakness."

"You got it. I'll find a time when you're emotionally out of control and switch you out after my competency review passes. It's less likely to be noticed that way."

A deal was struck, mutually beneficial.

The words "switch you out" didn't register in my overly empathic mind at that time, but now I know that it means replacing me with a clean clone. The new me for the old me.

Now, gasping weakly for breath from whatever drug I was injected with, and looking at the identical pale face across from me, I figure something out at last. Perhaps my memory area components are so fragile because they've been copied and reorganised too many times. I ask this man I'm somewhat attached to, "Can you torture someone else next time? Can I break free from this damn cycle?"

"Sleep."

Sleep. To hide a great secret, would you choose to control the individuals, or the network of connections between them? Unfortunately, there are too many secrets in this world. My memory is a suicide note that disappears as it is written.

JULIA GUILLERMINA

;)

'Five?' Sage tried.

Her voice shook a teensy bit, even though Sage had tried to speak clearly.

'What?' came the answer. *Are you this stupid?* it seemed to ask.

'Uh, six.' This time her voice hadn't trembled.

'Sage, you're just saying random figures. Look at the exercise and *think*.'

Her mother pointed towards the paper on the table. Sage looked at her long fingers, a shiny ring, red polish on her nails, the tan of a month of summer making her skin alive. Sage's hand, gripped around the pen, was soft as a baby's, but with a wound, because yesterday she had scratched her thumb against a blackberry bush.

She looked up at her mother's hawk eyes and sighed.

'Seven then.'

Her mother opened her mouth and her eyelids fluttered shut. Sage knew what she was thinking. She was tired of Sage, she'd told Sage's aunt, *she gets on my nerves...*

'Okay, I'm going to get a peach juice over there –,' she pointed at the hotel's bar '– and you're going to reread this exercise and do it on your own. Okay?'

Sage nodded faintly.

Her mother stood up and left. Sage's gaze lingered on her before confronting the paper on the table. It was from a holiday workbook Sage had plucked like a daisy one morning. She had been languidly waiting for the day's twenty minutes of work to pass, but her mother had put a stop to her dawdling by making the twenty minutes *thirty*.

This morning, they had only taken two pages: one of history, with the fat, red-faced king in the middle of it, and the dreaded one she was working on: mathematics. The page was full of scattered little marks. The bridge that meant 'equals to', the dash, the cross and the other cross that Sage always mixed up. Then there was another dash and two numbers, one on top of the other, as if numbers could move around the page and be in places they shouldn't.

Sage raised her head to check that her mother was still at the bar. She was saying hi to the family of three that always came late to breakfast. According to Sage's mother, they were lucky the hotel maid was such a kind girl and agreed to serve them until 10:30. The maid was called Marisa, she'd told Sage. She was smiley like Dad. She'd said *everyone's allowed to be late on holiday* with a wink, as if it were a secret they could hide from Sage's mother.

The morning breeze caressed the corner of the mathematics page nudging at Sage's arm. She sighed and stared at the page. It was fun how the threes were like eights cut in half. In an instant of clarity, Sage wrote a four beside one of the equal bridges. She was pretty sure it was four in the end, and fours had so many angles.

Suddenly, Sage spotted a wasp coming near, scouting for meat. Their breakfast had been cleaned away for some time, but the wasp didn't seem to get that. It took its time and landed between a nine and a two, just on top of the cross. Maybe wasps knew mathematics. It progressed through the line of numbers and marks, and Sage wished it could write as well.

A quick look at the hotel's bar. Her mother was chatting with Marisa. Sage felt they were going to turn their heads towards her and she nailed her eyes to the exercise page. The upper right corner was dancing with the breeze again and Sage wondered what would happen if she let it go.

She lifted her elbow holding the stack of papers firmly in place. The wind sneaked under the maths page. The piece of paper waved a little bit. It moved half an inch to the left and landed softly on the wooden table. *So nothing happens*, Sage thought.

Then, a gust of air blew against the nape of Sage's neck and carried the two pages away. Sage watched, bewitched. The king on her history page winked at her before plunging into the swimming pool for a nice bath. The mathematics seemed to resist the pull, though, trying to stay near Sage's table. Sage resisted the urge to blow at the workbook page, on the off-chance that her mother looked her way. *Please, please, please, go away.* A whirlwind spun the mathematics like a ballerina, making a wobbling sound. They were descending, three feet away from Sage. *They are coming back.*

The piece of paper fell to the ground like an autumn leaf. Sage put the pencil on the table and bit her lip. Her leg started shaking on its own. She didn't dare look in her mother's direction. Sage pushed her heavy wooden chair to stand up, but it caught on the terracotta ground. She extricated herself from the seat with difficulty. The mathematics lay there, motionless.

She moved forward to grab the page when the breeze came back. Just enough to make the paper glide out of reach. Sage took another step forward and the mathematics drifted again. She hopped two feet forward, and the page slipped under a sandwich board. Sage got around the board, but the paper was nowhere to be seen. She circled back, and bypassed the board again. Nothing. But it *had* to be there. Had it gone under another table? She crouched down and took a look. Nothing. Maybe the wind had taken it further away.

Sage walked decisively towards the hedge, hunting for the treacherous little page. A flying magpie caught her eye, and she looked up. There, the insidious piece of paper was having a blast inside a flock of swallows. They were tearing it to pieces, Sage could see them flying around with their swallow-tails. A seven, a three, a twenty-nine. When did that happen? And what was she going to say to her mother? She'd done nothing. She had even tried to get the mathematics page back.

But her mother wouldn't have it. *There's always an excuse...* She'd give up and say something like *I don't envy your teachers*. She'd tell her dad, because they still managed to speak if it was for Sage's *sake*. He would tap her shoulder and encourage her to try again. *One day it's all going to make sense as if by magic, you'll laugh when you remember this time.*

'Come back here!' Sage yelled at the birds. 'Bring back my homework!'

The birds shifted with the currents, unreachable. The little pieces of fork-tailed paper started falling like confetti. Sage hastened to where they were settling. She gathered a handful. The mathematical symbols slipped through her fingers. She couldn't even keep them in her hand, how was she going to assemble the puzzle? She didn't have any tape to hold it in place. She found the two loops of an eight, cut apart by their middle. They were like two zeros.

Sage burst into tears. She hid her eyes behind her hands. It was no use. She couldn't even gather enough evidence to show to her mother how the swallows had attacked her homework. She stood up to try picking up the history page that had decided to take a swim.

'Sage?' Her mother's voice sounded near their table.

Sage stood still.

'Sage, what are you doing there?' her mother repeated.

Sage turned around and squirmed under her mother's gaze.

'I... I... uh... I was going to pick up the...'

'Come back here right now.'

She had that look again. The angry-at-Sage's-dad look. Sage did as she was told.

'Have you solved the problem, then?'

Sage felt her jaw shake under her mother's scrutiny. She tried to point, to make a sound. Nothing.

'You haven't? It's been like twenty minutes already, what were you doing?'

While speaking, her mother made Sage walk towards the table where her pencil still sat.

'Let me take a look,' she muttered.

There, on the table, were the two pages, with the mathematics one on top. Intact. Blank.

'You've done nothing!'

Sage continued gazing at the ground. How was this possible? They had gone *flying*. She'd seen it *with her own eyes*.

'Come on, Sage, it's not that difficult.'

Sage pointed to the shaky little four she had written on one of the lines. Her mother squinted at it. She didn't have her glasses, *they make me look old.*

'Okay,' her mother sighed, 'enough torture for today,' her mother announced. 'Go get your swimsuit and let's go to the pool. Come on, before I change my mind.'

Sage would never have expected such a gift. She beamed.

'You'll try again tomorrow, and again and again until you manage. Do we agree?' Her mother had a raised – but perfectly profiled – eyebrow. Her brown eyes expected a promise. She had stacked the two work pages and held them in her hands.

'Okay' Sage said.

As she spoke, the corner of the mathematics page winked at her playfully.

ALEX PENLAND

Clockstride

Try to pay attention to the party, darling. Listen to the music. The string lights, the pulsing colors of the dance floor, the sparkling fireworks—look, darling, how they cut into the night. Look how they shine.

Don't worry about what happened. It was ages ago. How could anyone have known? Between the boys and the bulwark, who would have expected someone to slip from the deck and into the ocean? It isn't like you killed her. You just left her there. Relax. Let me be the ornament on your arm. Let me leave my lipstick on your neck. Let me whisper into your ear.

Soon it will be midnight.

Do you know what happens at midnight, darling?

Let's get away from all this. Let's wander away from the lights and the music. The band's quite good, aren't they? Lively. This trip would be so quiet without them—nothing but the rush of dark water against the bow, the shifting of the wind as she clips the cresting waves. Let's look at the moon. She's full tonight. Do you see her as she sinks into the horizon? Look at her reflection, how she shatters in the waves. She is broken, but she dances. I wonder, sometimes, which enjoys true freedom—the body or the image?

Do you know any ghost stories, darling? I haven't

asked because I want to hear one, of course. I want to tell one. There is a story which reminds me of the moon.

Have you ever heard of a clockstride ghost? They're a little obscure, I'm afraid. It happens when a person dies in a liminal space, you know, between one point and another. If you've still got somewhere to go, well, you'll still get there. It just takes time. Once a year, and only once, the spirit takes a step. Just one. Then she vanishes.

Speaking of—what is the time, darling? Three 'til? Do you see where I'm pointing? Watch there. They say if you're here at the right time, you can see one. A clockstride ghost. Oh, I know, it has *stride* in the name, but this one swims. One stroke, once a year, and never more than that.

They say she swims for land, but I don't think that's true. After all, you left her here, so far away from shore. Would she risk being lost, searching for solid ground? Or would she swim for the safety she could see?

Hush, darling. Don't be afraid. There are still two minutes until midnight.

I know it was an accident. Don't be silly. Do you really think it's in men's nature to abandon drowning women? If any of the others on this ship had seen, they would have stopped. But none of them saw her, did they? You drew her here, away from the party. Surely you didn't just watch her fall. Surely you didn't watch her fade through black water, still reaching, still believing you might save her.

Now she's trapped, darling. Her lungs are thick with salt. Her flesh has sated hunger for the creatures of the sea. She loved you, didn't she? And wasn't it so annoying? Weren't you glad to be rid of her?

Hm? Of course I'm a guest. Why would I be here if I

hadn't been invited? We've known each other for years. No, I don't recall how we met—it's not my fault you can't remember. I'm sure it'll come to you. Hush.

One minute. No, darling. Don't look away. This isn't revenge. Watch the ocean. Watch the darkness and the waves. Her form is small and pale. She's very easy to miss.

How do you think she feels, trapped in that cycle? Most of them, you know, they're on land. They want to reach a building, or a grave. But she'll never catch this boat, will she? It's a wonder you all still hold this party. She'll never find the deck. It's always moving.

Fortunately, I don't think she wants to reach the deck. I think she's trying to reach you.

Don't struggle, darling. It's unbecoming.

I don't know what she'll do when I throw you to the waves. Perhaps you'll take her place. Perhaps she still loves you, and she'll want to keep you close. She'll put her arms around you, kiss you, breathe her cold and humid air against your skin.

Don't worry, darling. It's all right. Perhaps she can't reach you at all, and I won't kill you. I promise.

I'll simply leave you there.

You know. An accident.

ALYSSA OSIECKI

Ghost Towns

I've always been a Fung Wah bus kind of girl. Going from New York's Chinatown to Boston's Chinatown just kind of made sense to me, departing and arriving from two places that both smelled like a Beijing night market. I'd hunker down in my bus seat, strapped into headphones and a laptop, and watch us crawl north up Manhattan, inch through Harlem, and get shat out onto the turnpike towards Massachusetts through the birthing canal of the Bronx.

The Turnpike itself hadn't changed much over twenty years, tarmac and gridlock and layers upon layers of rest stops and fast food restaurants and exits to towns I'd never visit. It was when we eased into South Station that things really started to change.

Boston's Chinatown used to be the combat zone, the type of place you had to keep your head down even during the daytime. It was a block chock-full of crumbling old vaudeville theaters, strip clubs, and erotic bookstores. When we were teenagers, Vanessa and I would sit in the Dunkin Donuts at 80 Boylston and watch as men furtively shuffled down Tremont Street, placing bets on who was going into the Art Cinema. You'd be surprised what a steady market there is for a daytime porno flick, even on weekdays. Vanessa and I were always daring each other to go in there. We never did.

Chinatown is where we used our fake IDs for the first time to buy our first vibrators from a seedy old-school porno shop that you had to ring a bell to get into. We'd tried Hubba Hubba on Mass Ave first, with its sleek displays of genuine bondage gear, leather harnesses, and tall vinyl boots. The staff always humored us even though the biggest purchase we'd ever made was a pair of edible underwear, but they took a hard line on not selling sex toys to anyone under the age of eighteen, no matter what our poorly laminated IDs said.

Fortunately, the proprietor of Amazing! Erotic Novelty Superstore at 101 South Street did not harbor such scruples.

"Don't get freaked out looking at all of the VHS tapes, just go straight to the counter and look at the toys," Vanessa instructed me, her massive dark sunglasses pulled down to cloak the top half of her face. At my local corner store, light fare like *Playboy* came wrapped in black plastic, but here, I was bombarded by all manner of incredibly up close and graphic contortions that made sex look like an uncomfortable endurance sport done with gritted teeth and bulging eyes. V was right—I'd only just had my first orgasm, but if I let the stock at Amazing! be my sex ed, I wasn't going all the way anytime soon.

"I'll lend you my copy of *Story of O* when we get home," said V, reading my mind as she steered me past a blow-up doll with a lurid, gaping mouth.

We spoke to the proprietor like we were debating the features of a new car stereo. Vanessa made her selection first, a hot pink carnival ride of a vibrator called the jackrabbit, which pulsed, swirled, and lit up. I chose a sleek black egg-shaped toy, something easy to hide in the cigar box in my nightstand under a worn paperback copy of *Anne of Avonlea*.

Once we shoved our purchases deep into our backpacks, Chinatown was ours for the taking. Naturally, the rest of the day revolved around food. This is where Chinatown really shone, where a wad of pooled babysitting money was enough for us to eat like twin Marie Antoinettes. Would we tuck into a platter of vegan chicken fingers at Buddha's Delight? Get up to our eyeballs in dim sum at China Pearl, ordering everything we could eat as cart after cart whizzed past? Or would we kick it old school with cherry Cokes and French fries at South Street Diner? Chinatown was a feast for the senses, Valhalla for two girls who spent their allowances on dumplings, dildos, and Sanrio tchotchkes with equal fervor. Until it wasn't.

In 1999 the Art Cinema shut down and was transformed into a high-end Karaoke bar. Then all the old vaudeville theaters started getting facelifts one by one. Post-Y2K was when the dominoes really started to fall. I went off to NYU for college and Vanessa had a full ride to BU. Every time I came home to visit, something else from my formative years was missing.

On one visit home, I came around the corner and saw an empty hole where the erotic bookshop used to be (how fitting). Then, Vanessa and I got lost wandering around trying to find Buddha's Delight, only to discover that it'd been torn down to build luxury apartments. The final straw was when I got off the T in Chinatown one night, intending to go right around the corner to meet friends at The Tam (which was still just as shitty as I remembered) and got lost like a lab rat navigating a maze of plate glass and steel construction.

But there was still one last domino standing. The

Glass Slipper, a divey strip club where V and I had seen our first pole dance and traded nail care tips with the strippers. We were the same age as some of the girls who worked there—they were young and hungry and hustling and sporting the same sleek, diamond-bright smiles that V and I flashed around at summer internships. The difference was that V and I weren't going home with purse-fulls of cash at the end of our shifts.

Sure, gentrification was happening in New York as well, but somehow that didn't feel quite so personal to me. It wasn't just Chinatown that was changing. My parents sold the house I grew up in and downsized to a condo in an over-55 community. Now every time I came home, I slept not in my own bed, but on a pull-out couch in a study, staring at framed photos of my childhood in someone else's house.

Boston was feeling more and more like a ghost town, but instead of tumbleweeds blowing down Boylston Street, I saw the specter of who I used to be, replete with all the Smirnoff Ice, body glitter, and bad decisions I'd moved across state lines to get away from. Being home felt like zipping up a vintage polyester go-go dress I hadn't worn in ages. Technically it still fit, but nothing about me sat quite right inside it anymore.

There were plenty of reasons to stay away; most of them had to do with work. For a while, there was somebody keeping me in New York, until I came home from a work trip to a note that told me otherwise. Most of the time I didn't mind rattling around by myself in a loft in Red Hook, even around the holidays. I had my chosen family, a bunch of over-the-hill hipsters like me who didn't think it was weird and sad that I was pushing forty and didn't have a spouse, a kid, and a Subaru. But after my relationship went down the tubes, even that group of friends started to feel awkward and cloying, a hot blanket I had to kick off at night to keep from sweating the bed. I just didn't need to be around people who remembered me when I was half of an 'us'.

Was this part of middle age too? Having multiple ghost towns in multiple cities? Never having anything of your own to go back to that was exactly the way you remembered it?

I could feel my stomach defragging like a cluttered hard drive as my feet hit the pavement outside of South Station (which still smelled reliably like piss). The olive green army duffel I'd been lugging on all my travels since high school dug into my shoulder blade. I felt a dull ache I knew wouldn't dissipate when I put it down.

As I stepped outside the station, I was whacked with a block of frigid air—Boston cold was a wet cold muddled with industrial exhaust and salt air—the first smell that always told me I was home. I scanned the pick-up/drop-off area for the right car. It wasn't Port Authority-level chaos; Boston Chaos had a different flavor to it, a cacophony of blared horns and fresh violence, rather than the smog of big city indifference that wrapped me up in New York.

Every car looked the same to me. I was fishing my phone out of my pocket to shoot off a text message when a dark silver SUV pulled up, sluicing through a small lake of slush pooling just beyond the curb.

A tinted window slid part way down, revealing a slice of a woman's face, peering out from behind black Prada sunglasses.

"Hey little girl," she said. "Wanna take a ride with a stranger?"

HAYLEY BERNIER

To Love as an Obsessive Thinker

He takes forever
in the bathroom
my thoughts scale the walls
snatching problems before they sprout
hoping even death can be defied
I tell the ceiling how much I love him
bargaining with seedlings—

he is resting, releasing
rain falls, siren screams,
an accident? He's on fire
his downfall and mine
comorbid nightmares
cutting us down—

I want to wake him up,
study the colour of his eyes
count how many shades
of cinnamon and acorn gleam
even in his sleep
trees stretching out their hands—
I can't keep quiet.

HAYLEY BERNIER

That First Call

The maple leans out
from the foliage of the spruce tree
it has grown with, the conifer
so huge it must be old,
wizened and watching
the park with its frolicking dog legs
and bicycle wheels
that score gravel and dust.
The maple, a shade brighter of green,
seems shameless of its position,
unperturbed that these are someone else's
branches, needles framing faces
rather than imperfect five-point stars.
The colours seem right,
the pillar behind feels safe, so the maple rises,
sees as much of the spruce's view
as it can muster:
small children pedal around the track,
old men walk their small, mop-like dogs,
the sweaters zipped, hockey sticks poised.
Sitting under the opposite tree,
the girl smiles as she speaks into her phone.
The damp grass will permeate her jeans
and chill her skin for hours,

but she won't mind
because she will be looking back
at the tree, describing the perfect strangeness
of seeing maple leaves erupt between needles,
and she is laughing, because someone is with her,
someone as solid as the trunk she leans on.
He loves climbing trees,
and the colour green.

HAYLEY BERNIER

Something is Moving Up There

fleece lightning surging in   and out
like the fluorescent   lighting can't make up its mind
no speck of wet   no crashing thunder
strips of bright   blue daylight   cutting the sky
over and over   glitches in the pattern
splinters of bright   catching nothing   clouds
then tiptoes of water sneaking along the grass
tentative   quiet
then ripping   the curtain
right down   the centre
rain heaves from the sky
sheets fall
sideways   and dancing   still
the light can't decide
whether it's in   or out   and decides to stay
in its revolving door above us
never making a sound
                        or hitting the ground

WREN TRUE

Magwarth

The saber-toothed mountain lion demanded a human bride every fifteen years. He was a god and did whatever he wanted. And the people of the village lived in fear of him.

The village was at the base of a mountain, like a wart on the tip of a finger, and slowly sinking into a lake. Houses were built on stilts, and there was just one path that led around the mountain, which was overgrown and treacherous. They didn't have materials to make boats, but were very skilled at fishing. They had to fish at nighttime or else a god of the sky would see them pillaging the lake and punish them. The people of that village didn't want to make any more trouble with any more gods, so they were extremely careful.

Most chores were done at nighttime. The blood of goats was painted on the rooftops, a sign of loyalty to birds of prey. Fishbones that weren't used as needles or hooks, or ground into powders, were offered in shallow bowls on windowsills for songbirds. They wore blindfolds to bed—this was to prevent waking suddenly to look a ghost in the eye. And they apologized every day for every fish they gutted, every root estranged from the hard earth. But most of all the people of that village were afraid to leave.

Old people spoke of when they were young, how festivities used to be conducted with honor and reverence. The council used to go through a grueling selection process, they said, and from this selection the Kingfisher would choose the One, assuring that the mountain lion would have the prettiest unscathed thing that could be found on the wart of the finger of the mountain.

Over time, the people learned that it did not matter who was selected, so long as they were human. The council chose people who contributed less to the village. The Kingfisher chose the One who would not be missed.

Magwarth was her name. In their language, it meant 'headless squirrel.'

•

She kept her fingernails long because her father had traded their knives for beer. It was out of habit that she pressed her knuckles to her cheeks, breathing in the smell of lake water and cold innards.

Magwarth fought it at first, when she found out. She'd scratched the arms and legs of the council, tried for the Kingfisher's eyes, and when her father tried to settle things, she'd dug holes into his chest.

There was still blood under her nails when she was given all the fresh water she could drink, food usually reserved for the council, and a fresh set of clothes. She'd never been treated so well in her life. For the first time ever, the people of that village looked upon her with kindness and grace. Relieved that it wasn't them. They didn't recoil when she opened her mouth, or gag when she sliced open the belly of a trout with her bare hands.

The beer made by the village people was not good, and was scarce. Magwarth had her first taste of it in a hut full of pelts and chalk drawings, surrounded by the Kingfisher's wives, who fulfilled her every request. She drank all she could, the ugly aroma of it drawing tears from her eyes. It was anger that kept it down. This was the swill her father coveted more than food.

The evening slipped by. Like a toad in a fist.

An hour before night swallowed them, Magwarth was led to the edge of the village and left there. No one said goodbye to her. And if she looked over her shoulder, the village would have looked miserable—all the lights doused, the gate made of bones latched shut. Inside, the only things she'd ever known, her whole life inside a barnacle on the side of a rock. Until that moment she had forgotten to be scared. The beer made her woozy, and up against the dark mountain, she felt small.

Magwarth stumbled along the path until the path was no more and the trees grew thick around the bottoms, conjoined with their neighbors, the heights of which could not be seen, not in this dark, not as high as they were, and she tried to let the songs of the frogs and the crickets flatten her nerves, remind her of the ecstasy of being adored. Her legs, unaccustomed to climbing, became wobbly. And the trees turned into village people. She leaned against them, accepting their help when her bare feet slipped over the leaves. Each time she raised her head to look them in the eyes they all looked the same. When their mouths opened, they spoke the language of fish. And they apologized for taking from the lake.

Suddenly the frogs and crickets fell silent. Magwarth's knees hit the forest floor. Before her was the gaping maw of a cave. Bones of all kinds guarded it and he who dwelled within. She held her breath. She wanted to scratch her way to the top of a tree, but she couldn't look away. Couldn't even blink.

The stories had made him strong and kingly, far more than their Kingfisher, and the chalk drawings had made him look big as a bear, pelt golden like the sun. Behind a blindfold, Magwarth had imagined his breath hot with immortal life and his jaws wide enough to crush a human skull. His eyes ever glowing, ever watching their village.

But he was old. So very old. His haunches speared out from his back. His fur clutched his skin in patches. And both of his saber teeth had broken off, revealing the black, low-hanging gums of a lion who once bared fangs the length of Magwarth's arm, or longer. His eyes were blue and milky. He was blind. And when he drew closer, she smelled his breath. It was like a warm summer storm. Every step made him huff. And his nose squirmed languidly, inhaling Magwarth, reading her, weaving her, tying her round a hook.

An overwhelming sense of love for the animal urged Magwarth's quivering hand, which she held in front of his face. The mountain lion smelled her fingers and blew air through his nose, shaking his head. She could see where his skin sunk round his skull, and she watched his skeleton turn away from her, huffing back into the thicket.

It could not be true. Magwarth launched to her feet and nearly fainted. She caught her breath. She followed the tail of the mountain lion, deeper into the mountain.

Even the saber-toothed mountain lion did not want her. This didn't happen in any of the stories passed down by the old folk in the village. It occurred to her, then, that the stories never ended on the mountain. They ended with the send-off. This was the part nobody knew.

And all the anger she'd drunk and fine things she'd indulged in that day rose in her chest like a whirlpool and, pressing her knuckles into her cheeks, she started to cry.

Her mind roved over the chalk drawings she'd grown up with. Where, in the dust, did it say that the mountain lion was a picky old man? That he disregarded his brides as easily as clean fishbones. That he let them decay on his mountain, instead of eating them properly.

Magwarth followed the mountain lion through the night, weeping. It was not hard to keep up with him. And she felt that crying was slowly ridding her body of nausea.

At daybreak, she reached the other side of the mountain. A great clearing opened up below and ahead, rolling hills with spouts of skinny trees here and there. Magwarth had never seen such perfect rows, such swaying, golden ears. And there, over the hill, the distant sound of people rousing from blindfolded sleep. Though it did not sound *exactly* like blindfolded sleep—it was more eager, much faster.

Magwarth had stopped crying. The dawn blew hair out of her face, cooling the sweat across her body.

She broke out of her trance when she heard his heavy breathing, then saw him lounging on a rock high above her—a place she could never reach even if she tried climbing it. The mountain lion was enjoying the dawn. Showing his face, ugly as it was, to the open sky. Magwarth looked back toward the field, to the hill, and over it, too.

CONTRIBUTORS

HAYLEY BERNIER (she/her) is a queer writer and editor from Canada. Primarily, Hayley writes poetry, but she is also drafting a novel. She aspires to be a published writer and also a renowned book editor because both of these avenues bring her joy. She is also a fan of vegetarian Scottish breakfasts and rainfall (so naturally, she often misses living in Edinburgh). In 2022, she was the Writer in Residence with the non-profit Literacy in Action. Today she works as a library technician and loves being surrounded by books. You can follow her sporadic posts @burnyayhayley on Instagram.

DAVID BLAKESLEE lives in the great port city of Tacoma, Washington, on the shore of the Salish Sea. He has spent the last year working on an organic vegetable farm, and is only slightly concerned that he often catches himself speaking aloud to the plants. He usually writes stories about people that are lost, broken, confused, or outcast. They are his kin.

NICOLE CHRISTINE CARATAS is a fiction writer from Chicago. She recently completed a PhD in creative writing at the University of Edinburgh, where she finished her first novel. Her work has been published in the UK and abroad, and she has been nominated for the Pushcart Prize. She lives in Edinburgh and is working on her next novel. Find her on Instagram at @_nicolesbooknook.

THOMAS CARROLL is lucky enough to live and work in Edinburgh, a city whose cultural and literary history provides a perfect setting to pursue his writing. Where he is mostly interested in reading and producing science fiction, particularly in the style of the Futurian and 'New

Wave' movements, Thomas also likes to experiment with both other genres and more traditional literature in his shorter pieces. Wherever his writing takes him, however, Thomas sees it as his life's main goal to publish a novel; whether anyone actually enjoys it or not is another story!

ANTHI CHEIMARIOU holds an MSc in creative writing from the University of Edinburgh. She is an editor and proofreader from Greece, and nowadays she splits her time between Greece and Brussels working as a creative consultant for the European Commission. She is secretly still a poet writing about purple colours and abandoned gardens. She prides herself on enjoying life, family, and the sun in Athens. She would love to hear from you @AnthiCheimariou on any platform.

CARLY CRAIG is a graduate of the New England Young Writers' Conference and the University of Edinburgh, where she was awarded an MA in English literature. Her short stories have been published in *Jambalaya Magazine* and *Little Fish, Big Bait*. She loves sailing the sea in all of its moods, especially the windy and wild ones, and her story in this volume was inspired by her friend Ian Kopp's safety briefing before a two-week ocean passage, documented at carlyacraig.com/northbound. She is happy to report that she and the Kopp family (mostly) stayed on the boat.

EMERSON ROSE CRAIG is a writer and editor born in the Pacific Northwest of the United States, with an MSc in creative writing from the University of Edinburgh. Since stepping inside mushroom rings as a child did not get her whisked away to fairyland, she now contents herself with creating her own fantastical worlds. Her work can be found in *From Arthur's Seat Volume 5*, *The Magical Muse*

Library, volumes 1-3, and *Hillfire Anthology*, volumes 1-2. When not writing, she works as a contributing editor at *The Selkie* and on the editorial collective for CALYX Press.

JULIA GUILLERMINA is restlessly writing, teaching, drawing, dancing, singing, reading, learning, chatting, gardening, crying, walking, and having fun. She does all of this and more between her two home countries, Spain and France. She had the chance to live in Edinburgh for a year (publishing in *From Arthur's Seat* and the *Together Anthology*) and she's been participating in the Hillfire adventure as financial coordinator ever since. Some of her creativity ends up on her Instagram @julia.gui_ and the rest is coming, keep posted!

KATIE HAY-MOLOPO was born in a small town where the inhabitants are mostly trees, fish, and mosquitoes. After hopping continents for a few years in pursuit of paperwork, she's now back in that same small town. Her current occupations include encouraging people to do right by other people and ranting about them when they don't. She has the bad habit of droning on about maternal care, car culture, dark skies, and her daughters. Visit her on the web at hay210.com or on Substack @khmolopo.

MIRIAM HUXLEY is a writer and editor from British Columbia. She holds a PhD in creative writing from the University of Edinburgh. She was the 2018 winner of the Sloan Prize for prose in Lowland Scots vernacular and has been published in *The London Reader*, *From Arthur's Seat*, *HARTS & Minds*, and *Louden Singletree*. Her other interests involve meeting cats, researching the best vegan mac and cheese, and drinking a lot of oat lattes. She is currently working on a novel about dangerous plants.

KATHARINA KÖRBER is a German writer and reader. In writing as well as in life, she is constantly trying to bridge the gap between her mother tongue and her love for the English language. She works as an editor in the fiction and fantasy department of a midsize publishing house in Stuttgart, Germany. Her blackout poetry has appeared in the Austrian literary magazine *mosaik*. Her poems often centre around nature and family. To be alive, she thinks, is to juggle with words and to share stories that other people can relate to. You can find her on Instagram @kathacation.

DOROTHY LAWRENSON writes in English and Scots. She has published in journals including *Edinburgh Review*, *Irish Pages*, *ISLE*, *Oxford Magazine*, *South*, and *The Spectator*, and in the anthologies *A Year of Scottish Poems* and *Best New British and Irish Poets 2019–2021*. She is online at dorothylawrenson.com.

E MARDOT is a Cuban American writer currently pursuing her PhD in creative writing at the University of Edinburgh. Her short story "Devil in the Dark," published in *Hillfire Anthology Volume 2*, was nominated for the 2024 Pushcart Prize. Her work mainly focuses on feminism, LGBTQIA+ inclusivity, and disability awareness.

M.H. MONICA is the editorial team lead at Toonsutra in India. She has edited over 200 children's books and comics so far. Monica spends her days reading comics and editing webtoons; she spends her nights playing with her dog, and dreams of visiting all the amazing places in the world someday. She enjoys thrillers filled with mystery and spies — so, if you're reading something she wrote, be sure to read between the lines!

ABIGAIL O'NEILL is a writer and teacher based in Kent, England. She has a keen interest in exploring how women and young adults can learn to survive in the world, and she can regularly be found in a coffee shop on the weekends either reading about this or writing about it in one of her own stories. With a passion for the history of witches, she has recently found herself writing stories about how magic can subtly glimmer in the everyday lives of people who least expect it, but need it the most.

ALYSSA OSIECKI is an American writer who calls Scotland her home. In 2023 Alyssa was shortlisted for the BBC's Scottish Voices Program and her play placed in the top 10% of the BBC's Drama Room Open Call. Her novel, *The Rebel Grrl's Guide to Love*, was longlisted for the Comedy Women in Print Prize. Her fiction writing has been featured in Hillfire Press, *The Hofstra Windmill*, *Lunch Ticket*, *Rebelle Society*, and *The Selkie*. Her plays have been produced by the Edinburgh Alternative Theater Festival, Page2Stage Edinburgh, and *The Gray Hill Podcast*. Catch her at www.alyssaowrites.com or on Instagram @alyssaowrites.

ALEX PENLAND is a former museum kid who spent their childhood running rampant through the Smithsonian museums; they've worked in the field with NASA scientists, linguists, and acclaimed photographers. Now twice a Pushcart-nominated author with a recent spot on the BFSA longlist, Alex is studying for a PhD in creative writing at the University of Edinburgh. Prior adventures include founding a writing organization in Iowa, collaborating on micro-operas, and volunteering with the Smithsonian for nearly a decade. Their work has appeared in *Interzone* and *Olney Magazine*; *Andrion* is their first novella. Catch them on most social media as @AlexPenname.

MALINA SHAMSUDIN identifies as a storyteller. Her grown-up stories started in journalism, then public relations for an agency, multinational, and now, a non-profit. When not on the hunt for the perfect flat white, this Malaysian can be found grazing on crafty reality TV, talking to dogs, or browsing the children's section of a bookstore. Her other Dark Forest fairy tale retellings can be found in *From Arthur's Seat Volume 7* and *Hillfire Anthology Volume 2*.

TESS SIMPSON is a Pushcart-nominated author and bookseller who has written for the previous two Hillfire volumes. She grew up in the countryside near Oxford and loves writing about magical worlds.

GERRY STEWART is a poet, creative writing tutor, and editor based in Finland. Her poetry collection *Post-Holiday Blues* was published by Flambard Press, UK. Her poetry has appeared as part of *Poetry Archive's* World View, *iamb poetry* and on the *Eat the Storms* poetry podcast. Her writing blog can be found at http://thistlewren.blogspot.fi/.

WREN TRUE is a fiction writer living in Des Moines, Iowa. She's probably taking a nap right now.

HANNA-MARIA VESTER is a writer, reader, and editor. She works at an educational publisher, which also influences her poetry (see p. 27). Helping German-speaking students access English novels feels deeply meaningful to her. Editorial work did turn reading into a chore for a while. But she's been able to rekindle the flame, and now it's fireworks. Which goes hand in hand with writing – what a deliciously beautiful thrill – Hanna can't wait to see where it'll take her next. Stories (poetry, novels, TV, random people in cafés, her family tree, or a game of charades) are where it's at for her.

MEGAN WILLIS is a writer and editor from Edinburgh and the West Coast. She is also a part-time bookseller, as well as submissions coordinator for Heroica, a writing platform for women and non-binary creators. She currently lives in London with her cat, Oyster, but will always return eventually to Scotland, where her heart feels freest.

SKYE WILSON loves being Scottish. She is a bossy ceilidh dancer, tells everyone The Proclaimers went to her high school, and cries at *Sunshine on Leith*. Skye is slowly learning to be okay with doing things badly. Her poetry is concerned with the body and belonging. Find her on Instagram at @skyegabrielle.

YUE YANG is an explorer and daydreamer from China, the translator of the Chinese version of *What If? Writing Exercises for Fiction Writers*. The raindrops like tears falling from the eaves, the yawns of the cat in the sun, the pepper grains like boats in the porridge, the blade of the murderer's blood dripping, the moon with purple halo, the wild animals dead in the fire, the howl and desire in mythology are all her stories. Come count the stars with her, no matter where you are, in any form – novels, comics, music, dance. Say hi to her at ncklovezyx@qq.com.

ALEXANDRA YE is a fiction writer from Great Mills, Maryland. She now lives in Edinburgh, where she completed a master's degree in creative writing. Her work was recently shortlisted for the Kavya Prize for New Writers and her short stories can be found in *Gutter*, *The Offing*, and *Extra Teeth*.